CAPTURED

K. A. BRYANT

"…Without God, we can do nothing…" John 15:5
Grateful for the ability to do what I love.
Be a wife
Be a mother
Be a daughter.
Be a writer.
Thank you to my dear husband for your continuous support.
This book is dedicated to you.
To my wonderful children, words couldn't express how full
My life is with you.- I love you!
Mom & Dad, God bless you and thank you for all your support.

CAPTURED

CHAPTER ONE

Tempest Bleu

The champagne-soaked hotel carpet, cold and matted beneath my bare feet. What day is it? I feel as though I have been here forever. How long have I been standing? My heels ache. I release my grip, feel my fingernails pull out of my palm and Christian's handkerchief fall to the bed. I need to sit.

What was that? My foot bumped the empty champagne bottle on the floor and it rolls, stopping against platform beneath the beige bed. I shouldn't have drunk. I haven't since our wedding day twenty-five years ago today so my head is spinning. My smeared mascara is dry and tight on my face. My eyes sting and are so puffy it's hard to keep them open. Where is it? What did I do with it?

The card from the Embassy Agent. A crooked toupee. That's all I remember. Doug-something...his toupee hung too far left... what is his name? I rub my forehead then toss the covers on my side of the bed. Nothing.

Christian's side is still made. I won't ruffle it. I smooth my hand over his cool pillow. The pillow, where his head would have lain last night if it weren't for me. There is blood on the back of my hand and everything is such a blur.

"Why haven't the Police called yet?" I mutter aloud.

The man at the embassy said they would call...come by...I can't recall now. Finally, the phone rings.

"Ouch!" My fake nail pops off as I grab the telephone receiver.

"HELLO! Christian?"

"Mrs. Bleu, this is Janet from the front desk."

"Oh."

"I'm calling to let you know that the last evacuation bus is leaving for the airport in five minutes. It has been highly recommended that all Americans-"

"NO! I'm not leaving!" Conviction. Immediately I feel it. I should not have yelled at her. She's only doing her job. I take a deep breath. "No, I'm sorry..." I rub the back of my neck, and strands of my hair, now droopy curls fall over my right eye, "...I will be staying, thank you." I hang up the phone agitated.

Gunshots. Still more? I jump, with every shot. My top is moist with perspiration and my right sleeve is torn. My body shaper undergarment is squeezing me terribly. Secondary, to my other problems.

Someone should have come by now. Douglas's toupee

leaned while he said he'd send the Police. How can they let this go on?

Our passports are still on the bare desk beside my broken perfume bottle. Christian would put them in the safe. I grab them, throw them into the open safe and slam it shut and hurry back to my position on the bed beside the phone. I feel safer here. Close to where he would have lain.

Our suitcases still stand in the corner side by side. We didn't even get a chance to unpack. I can't help but feel guilty. Why did I do it? Why! I rub my eyes and feel fresh tears slip between my fingers. This reality melts away behind the champagne and I open my eyes in my safe place. Home.

Earlier That Day

It's bright. Without question, this is my favorite place in our home. The octagonal glass sun-room warmed by the sunlight pouring in. The view of the half-acre garden seems to go on forever.

The cathedral ceiling makes me feel small. Perhaps that's why I enjoy this room so. The callous-handed gardener is pruning the rose bushes. With the press of a button, I lower a shade blocking light falling directly on my freshly made-up face.

I raise my warm cup of tea to my lips and the sound of water running from the indoor fountain is remarkably relaxing.

"Mrs. Bleu, which luggage would you like to use?"

"The Louis Vuitton. Set them out, will you Doris, I'll be up in a second. Have you arranged the outfits I requested as yet?"

"Yes, Mrs. Bleu. But you still need to select your delicate items."

Doris is a dear. Though only a few years older than I, she thinks like me and I thank God she has a sense of humor. She is discreet. By personal items, she means my girdles and shaper-wear.

"If it snaps like a slingshot, put it in the suitcase, Doris. I need all the help I can get. And Doris, no swimsuits. Let's spare mankind that one."

Doris takes a tissue from her white apron pocket, dabs her nose, trying to hide her smile as she walks away. I found having a sense of humor, a natural buffer when I grew to my voluptuous size.

Doris clears the tea tray, and I enter Christian's office. He hangs up the phone and is pensive. Too pensive. I turn to face him.

"McLean?" I ask knowingly.

"McLean." He nods.

"You do all the work. It's you who the clients request time after time. He's become bitter, Christian. I saw it when we had him and his *girlfriend* over for dinner. I don't like the way he looks at you and you know-"

"-Yes, I know, 'you are usually right'. I think you started hating him when he broke up with Terry. She left *him*, you know."

Christian puts his hands in his pockets. I like those khaki shorts on him. And he's finally wearing the loafers I bought him three months ago.

"Your legs are sexy," I say lightly.

He looks down at them.

"You're biased." He says.

"So?"

"He's my college buddy-"

"-was your college buddy. Now he's a bitter, jealous man who you can't trust. See him for what he is, not what he used to be."

"You're smart." He says.

"Your biased," I say.

"True." He says.

I take his hand and squeeze it tightly.

"He said he'll sign when we get back from our trip. Remember to tell no one where we are going. For security reasons." He says as I walk out of the room. "I already registered the trip with the United States travel Department. Can never be too safe." He says.

"My man." I throw him a kiss as I leave the room and humorously do my happy dance feeling his brown eyes on me. "The car is ready. We leave for the airport in twenty minutes." I yell back at him, hurrying to see what Doris has packed.

I hear him laugh. I've done my job. The phone in his office rings. Why isn't he answering it?

Present Day

Wait, that is here, now. In the empty hotel suite dotted with white roses, he ordered. I push my hair back and eagerly grab the phone.

Suddenly, I'm afraid. What if it's the detective with some hideous news? Wait, what if it's Christian? My warm memory vanished.

"Christian?" I say softly.

"What? Is this Mrs. Tempest Bleu?" says a male voice.

"Yes, this is Mrs. Bleu... I'm sorry I can barely hear you." I say.

Police sirens and gunshots sound outside the hotel window quite loudly, despite our room being on the fifth floor.

"Mrs. Bleu, this is Hannraoi." He says.

"Who?"

"Mr. Douglas, from the United States Embassy. You came to see me earlier- "

"-Yes. Do you have any news?"

"Has he contacted you?"

"No, nothing. No calls... no, he's still not answering his cell phone. He always answers my calls, always! I told you, he's consistent, reliable. What have you found! Tell me you found something. PLEASE!"

"Mrs. Bleu, please calm yourself. I need you to listen to me closely. You came to see me through all of that chaos earlier and by some miracle, you weren't killed in the process. The rioting is increasing and expected to get worst. You-"

"-What has that got to do with this?" I can't stand listening to him drone on. Normally, I wouldn't mind, but I want answers.

"You must not attempt to come to the embassy again. Do you understand me?" he says.

"Yes. all right."

"I will be in contact with you via telephone. Your cell phone, preferably. I don't know if you have been watching the television, or how good your Spanish is but, all American's have been advised to leave the country immediately."

I look at the television I turned on earlier. It's on mute. I didn't want to hear it. I wanted to see the news just in case anything about Christian being found came on. I'm listening to him but can't help but wildly scan the room, not seeing any of it. This doesn't feel real. It may just be the champagne or it may be the stress. I don't know. This feels surreal.

Now, I feel it. I feel his absence. I feel the loss of his buffer. He shields me. All the time, he shields me from pain, stress, all of it. He has this way, I can't explain it. A touch. A hug, a glance or smile. It buffers the rough edges of life. Now, there is nothing between me and fear. I feel all of it.

"I'm not leaving!" I never yell. My life in the church and within my sanctuary didn't mandate it. But it feels good. "I told you that, in the office yesterday. I will not leave Mexico without my husband. If I have to, I will go out there and search by myself... I will!"

I wipe my eyes with the bottom of my shirt. They are the same clothes I wore on the plane.

"Mrs. Bleu, you will not be helping your husband if you get yourself killed. I also need to advise you to look at this from another perspective.

I have seen men, at a certain age... well come out here and get involved with, well... someone else and start a new life but leave their wives, well... the ability to collect insurance money to put it frankly. They see it as a way to help deal with the guilt. I just want you to know that if a man does not want to be found, we will not find him. Your husband, as I understand it, is a man with very special and extensive means so-"

What is he saying? I got lost in the news showing cars being set on fire, American flags being burned and people shooting guns in the street.

"-Mr. Douglas, they took my husband. He's a dedicated Christian. I told you, we got off the plane. We missed the hotel bus and took a taxi."

14

The car was so small, not like American taxi's, I can still feel his body pressed against my left side, and mine against his right.   It was warm. Very warm, despite the air conditioning in the car.

"As you saw from the photo, he is a big man. We match in every way- "

"-Which is why it is odd that someone would select him to kidnap."   He interrupts.

"You don't understand, we had plans.   Right after this trip, we were going on a diet, together. We joined a gym just before we left. Does that sound like someone not planning to return? We do everything together. Everything. We even bought matching walking sneakers.
Mr. Douglas will be honest with you. I am a little drunk, but I assure you, my husband would never have picked up the champagne bottle.
He doesn't yield to temptation or bow to pressure.   He is strong.   He is true.   I wish I was more like him."   I wipe my nose with the back of my hand and my wedding ring stays in my gaze.
"He made a vow to me twenty-five years ago today and we came here to... (I swallow) ... rededicate our marriage. If you don't believe in my husband, you can't help us."

"I want to find your husband, Mrs. Bleu. As I said earlier coming to the embassy would be futile because we have shut down for safety reasons.   Listen, it has been three days since Christian went missing-" he says.

"-it seems longer."

"We may need to wait until things have resolved out there before our search can start. The Mexican Police are overwhelmed right now. That's why no one has contacted you. But, they know and will send someone to you as soon as possible."

"Mr. Douglas, it's time to go." I hear someone say in the background of his office.

I want to throw the phone across the room. But I can't.

"Thank you, Mr. Douglas. I understand, "I say. I'm lying. I don't understand, but that's the nice thing to say.

I hang up the phone, feeling more alone than before I answered it. I need to go to the bathroom. But not without his handkerchief. I search for it and pick it up from the bed. I raise it to my face and take a deep breath. It smells of his cologne.

In the taxi on the way here, I remember how the sun shone on his face. His eyes tightly closed. I dabbed his perspiration with the handkerchief, then slipped my hand around his forearm. His arms, strong, muscular and quite intimidating to those who don't know his gentle heart. His tooth aching unbearably. Knowing his high tolerance to pain so, I'm concerned.

The senior taxi driver was kind. His tan, creased skin and coarse hands gripped the steering wheel firmly while he glanced at us in the rear-view mirror.

I still recall trying not to laugh as he opened his mouth as wide as he could to show us his teeth. The handiwork of the dentist he was recommending us to.

My husband is usually reluctant to go to doctors, so when I saw his willingness to drop our luggage at the hotel and have the taxi driver take us directly to his dentist before they closed, I knew this was severe.

I'm missing something. I can't help but run this through my mind over and over again. But if I don't figure it out, who will? The toupee won't. Christian will be left with no one to help him. I have to figure this out. The champagne isn't helping.

The light in the bathroom is coldly honest. It reveals everything. My quarter-sized birthmark on my neck is redder than usual. It gets that way when I get upset or my blood pressure is high. My pills are in my purse. Christian. Dear Lord, he doesn't have his pills, or does he? I paw through a few of our items on the sink we left in haste earlier. He doesn't have them. I shake the bottle and it's full. He's supposed to take it once a day. I completely forgot about them. My raw reflection is daunting.

This bright bathroom light accents every fold in my chin, every overhanging cheek, and crease. My hair doesn't look as if I had it done at all. The result of my insatiable habit of pushing it back when I'm thinking. The last eight hours I pushed it back constantly. Until I drank the champagne. I feel breathless and my heart just won't stop racing.

"Relax, breathe." That's what Christian says to me when I'm like this. For some reason, it doesn't have the same effect when I say it to myself.

I wish I were fitter now, more agile. More athletic. What if I have to run to get out of here? Except for Jeff and Nancy next door, the hotel is probably empty. I saw people leaving by the busloads from my window overlooking the front of the hotel. From inside my bathroom, I heard talking through the wall about an hour ago. So, at least they are still here.

I feel clearer after washing my face. I tie my hair back into a sloppy ponytail. I got highlights put in my dark hair thinking it would make me look younger.

I desperately wanted this second honeymoon to be special. I planned to be at my goal weight for it, but well, as usual, I didn't stick to my diet. Christian doesn't care about my weight at all. 'You're beautiful', I recall him saying when he saw me turning away from the mirrors quickly like I am now.

I need to think. I look at my makeup case on the right and Christian's toiletry bag on the left. What if Mr. Douglas and his crooked toupee were are right? What if Christian left me? Is it impossible? Unthinkable?

Reluctantly, I look in the mirror again. I don't look like that bride he brought here twenty-five years ago. I can't remember the last time I slipped into a negligee. Perhaps he was just being kind. What if, he needed someone... better? He did go to many business social dinners alone. He said it was because of his line of work; he didn't want to give anyone accesses to his personal life. It was for my protection, so he said.

His zipped leather case is staring at me like a bag of clues. I never go into that case. He packs it himself, always. But why? Now that I think about it, I asked him if he wanted me to pack it for him and he took it from me saying he would do it. Why?

If I open it, I don't trust him. I will never drink again. It's making me crazy. I walk out of the bathroom and shut the door behind me. I know him. I leave his toiletry case untouched.

What is that banging? Is it the police? I rush to the hotel room door. No, it's not on my room door. I peek through the peep-hole. It is that woman again. The loud one from the plane banging on the door next door.

Why is she bothering Jeff and Nancy? We all saw her on the plane. We had no choice. She sat across the aisle from Christian and I and spent boarding time cursing out someone on her cell phone. Christian said flying commercial draws less attention, especially when going into Mexico. I missed the quiet of a private flight thanks to lady loud-mouth. That wasn't nice. That thought isn't like me. Then again, this whole day isn't like me.

I didn't think to ask Jeff or Nancy if they saw Christian. I need to. I need to do something besides sit here concocting theories. Why aren't they answering the door for her? I fix my large flowing shirt, slip on my flats and tap on the door connecting our room to Jeff and Nancy's.

"Jeff, Nancy? Are you all right? It's me, Tempest."

I hear someone moving. Then the door lock clicks, but no one opens it. I wait a few moments then turn the nob and push. The door opens. I hope they don't realize that I'm half drunk.

Someone is sitting on the floor in front of the sofa in the suite's sitting room. Short blond hair, fresh cut. Clean shaved. It's Jeff.

Bouquets of white roses stuffed into glass vases top every table in the room and rose petals scattered on the bed and floor. An evening gown still on its hanger is draped across the foot of the bed with a pair of new matching shoes on the floor beside the bed.

"Jeff?" I say, walking around the sofa to him.

At this moment, I forget my pain. I step into his world. Why is he on the floor? I turn and face him. His knees are up and he is resting both his elbows on them with his hands cupping the top of his head.

His television is on the news as well, with the volume as loud as it can go, drowning out the police sirens and gunshots along with the rude woman's banging.

"Jeff? Are you- " I begin and what I see makes me stop.

I take a step backward. There is fresh bright red blood splatter on his white dress shirt. His cuffs are folded up to the elbows, but I can see blood through the folds and dried blood beneath his nails.

Ministry. A switch in my head flips. In the church, I'm in charge of a grief counseling. They started the group right after 9-11.

None of it worked for me last night. I broke every rule I taught. But seeing Jeff like this, it all kicks in again.

His eyes are locked on a splatter of blood on his dress shoes and I'm surprised he opened the door at all for me.

"Jeff, can you hear me?" I asked, bending down to his seated level.

I reach for the remote to turn down the television.

"No." He says. "They may show Nancy."

He looks up at me as if he's in shock. He spins his wedding ring, the corner of his mouth still bleeding and the white of his right eye, bloodshot. He was beaten up badly. A satellite phone is on the floor beside him, rings. He looks at it, closes his eyes for a moment, then answers it.

"Dad."   Says Jeff.

An explosion outside rocks our hotel. Squatted, I lose my balance and end up seated on the floor. His Dad is speaking so loudly I can hear him ask 'what was that'?

"What was what?"   Jeff says to his dad.

Jeff didn't even hear the blast.   He puts the phone down on the floor and presses speakerphone.   Does he know I'm here?

"Son, I am arranging your transport out of there. The private plane is on the way.   It will bring you to us in Massachusetts. We will sort this out, here."

"Why dad?"   asks Jeff.

"Why, what son?"

"Why did they kill her?   But they let me go?   I don't get it.   I'm the one with money."   He says bluntly.

"No one knows, son.   When you get here, we will sort it out.   I have arranged private security for you. Two armed guards will come get you at the hotel.   Don't leave the room until they get there.   Do you hear me?... Jeff? Don't leave that room. They are taking Americans."

Jeff reaches over and hangs up the phone.   The loud woman is still pounding on the door.   Nancy, dead?   Oh, Lord.   I pray that's not what happened to Christian.

Now, the probability of death feels very real.   I feel invisible but privileged that he opened the door for me at all. I need to make sure he hears me.

"Jeff, I'm so sorry about Nancy," I say choking back tears.

He looks at me as if being drawn out of a dream and begins crying uncontrollably. Then he does something that comes from the core of humanity.

He opens his arms, reaching for me. His face crumbles into an agonizing grimace and hugs me. He's crying from his core. I fight to hold my tears back. Jeff's half my age. If I had a son, he would probably be Jeff's age. He's pouring out his pain.

I have that effect on people.   They see me and just start gushing what hurts them. I soak it up like a gauze. I don't get it, but I think it's a blessing.   He sits back and wipes his face with his sleeve.   I didn't ask, but he tells me what happened.

"We were coming back from visiting friends, right in front of the hotel," he extends his hand, "when they grabbed us.   They threw us in a van and took off.   It happened so fast.

They drove us somewhere. It felt like forever. They separated us then," he takes a breath, "they brought her to where they were holding me and... they made me watch! They wouldn't let me... look away. They cut her throat. I couldn't do anything," his arms drop to his sides limp, "Tempest! Nothing! They let me go so I could hold her. She died in my arms." He holds out his arms as if he were cradling her.

The bloodstains on his shirt and pants match the way he cradled her head.

"They shoved me back in the car and drove me back here and pushed me out. She's still there. Alone." His voice wavering.

I swallow and feel my stomach turn. I jump up and run to the bathroom and vomit all the champagne into the toilet. My Christian. He's still out there. Is that what happened to him? Is he alone?

I hear him stand and the clank of a whiskey flask on a thick stocky glass. I rinse my mouth and wash my face again.

"I know you hear me!" yells the rude lady still outside the door.

I pause in the bathroom doorway, watching Jeff go to the door from the corner of my eye.

"Go away!" he yells, turning up his glass.

"Please!   I know you have a phone.   I just need to use the phone.   I heard you talking-"

"-Get in your room stupid!"   yells Jeff.

"I can't.   I locked myself out.   Please, help me." She softens her voice.

I walk out of the bathroom and Jeff looks at me as if my response will determine his.   I nod.   He unlocks the door, and she hurries into the room.

"It's about time!   Where is it?   I need to call my husband."   She says curtly. "What are you people, deaf?" reaching for the television volume.

"Don't touch it!" yells Jeff.

"Whatever." She says.

She takes three seconds to look me up and down and roll her eyes. She is oblivious or heartless.   I don't judge people, I just have a gift of seeing their true selves.   The one they usually try to hide. She sees the blood on Jeff but asks nothing.   She's walking around the room and picking up things, seeing if the phone is beneath it and dropping them carelessly.

Jeff has the phone in his pocket and looks as if he has no intention of giving it to her.   The electricity has been blinking on and off all morning.

She turns to Jeff and sees the bulge in his trouser pocket. She's approaching him formidably.

"I'm Tempest, Tempest Bleu.   Mrs..."   I say extending my hand trying to quench the fire kindling. I give her an opportunity to tell her name.

She rolls her eyes at me, continuing to Jeff abruptly. She's in a bikini top and linen pant with very elaborate strapped sandals and an over-sized purse swinging from her bent arm.

"I said, I have to call my husband. I thought you were a gentleman. Pathetic room. I had to leave my penthouse because my cell phone died, so don't mess with me!"

Jeff ignored her until now. She pulls a cigarette from her large beach bag and lights it. He slaps it from her hand.

"Hey!"   she puts her hands on her hip.

"My wife doesn't like cigarette smoke."   He says. "Sit down, shut up or get out."

I would never have been bold enough to do that. I'm proud of Jeff.

"You don't know what's going on out there, do you?   The whole country has gone into disarray. Americans are the target because someone's genius in government did something.
I missed the last evacuation bus because I was swimming, but I need to get out of here."   Says the rude woman pointing to the door with her bright red fingernail

polish shimmering on her tips.

"They said we should stay in our rooms. That's the safest place." I say.

"What do you know about it? Go find a donut."

"Hey!" says Jeff. "One more crack like that and I'm putting you out of here, got it?"

She shirks her shoulders and plops down on the sofa with one leg beneath her.

"Haven't I seen you... the plane, right? You were with someone." She says to me.

Jeff turns and looks at me. He has come to himself and just realized I'm alone. Moist-eyed, he looks at me.

"Tempest?" he says.

It's funny, because of what he just went through, I feel him reading me. I don't want to divulge more than that, not in front of her. Jeff realizes it and turns away from me.

I feel her size six eyes traipsing all over me. Her hair looks great. A perfect cut and her ring finger indented from a ring. But no ring. Perhaps she took it off to swim. I'm sure it matches her large pink diamond stud earrings.

If Christian were beside me, I wouldn't feel so naked around someone like her. He's not. I don't want her to know but, what if she can help? What if she saw something? I can't let pride keep me from asking. I open my mouth to speak, and there is a loud, hard knock on the door.

Jeff looks at us and shakes his finger 'no' then puts his finger to his lips telling us to stay silent. The rude lady pops up from the seat wide-eyed and goes to the door, looking through the peep-hole. The loud television masks any noise from our movements.

"It's the police," the rude woman says.

"They were coming to talk to me," I whisper to Jeff.

Jeff puts his hand on the woman's shoulder, stopping her from touching the lock on the door. We all step away from the door.

"How do we know they are real?" Jeff says.

"I didn't think of that," I say taking a step back from the door. You're right. We can't open the door."

"Are you as nuts as you are fat? I said it's the Police, La Policia." She goes to the door and puts her hand on the lock.

"Hey, Tempest is right." He whispers. "We don't know if they are truly police officers. You open that door, you risk us all." Jeff exclaims pointing to the door.

"Maybe it's the two men your dad sent for you." She looks at her fingernails.

"How do you know about that?" asks Jeff.

"Heard it through the door." Jeff walks up to her. She reaches for Jeff's hair. He swerves his head, avoiding her touch. He looks as if he wants to hit her. I need to intervene.

"Wait, the hotel Manager said not to open the door for anyone until they made their official announcement." I back away from the door. "Don't open that door."

"We don't even know if there is anyone down there." She says. "I tried to call the front desk, no answer. For all we know, the hotel management is halfway to the border."

Jeff picks up the room phone and calls the front desk, then hangs up.

"No answer." He says.

"See. They are here to rescue us. It's in the registry where all the American's in the hotel are staying. Before I left, my husband registered my trip with the United States Passport office with my hotel room and everything.
He hasn't heard from me in twenty-four hours, he probably called them for me." She opens the door latch and puts her a hand on the deadbolt lock.

"You mean the husband you cursed out on the plane." I couldn't help it. It fell out of my mouth. She's about to put Jeff and me in danger.

"What did you say?" She takes her hand off the

lock and approaches me.

She looks like she could hit me with a yoga move or something. She wouldn't dare approach me like that if Christian were here. His very presence protected me. That's what I want her to do. That's right, lash out, get it off your chest. Just don't open that door.

"I didn't stutter," I say feeling my palms get sweaty.

"You nosy little- "

"Enough." Whispers, Jeff.

They moved. We hear them knock on my hotel room door. The rude lady is steaming angry. She grabs her purse, tightens her lips and runs through the open door connecting my room to Jeff's.

"No!" Jeff reaches for her, but she escapes his hand.

We hear her unlock the room door. Quietly, Jeff and I shut the connecting door, lock it from inside Jeff's room and press our ears to the wall facing each other… listening. Because she ran out of my room. Hopefully, they will assume she is alone.

"THANK GOD!" we hear the rude woman say to the officers in the hall.

"Ma'am, are you alone?" asks one officer in a

heavy Hispanic accent.

I tip-toe to the peep-hole in Jeff's door and lookout. I can see one officer walk into my room, roughly pushing past her. She walks into the hallway, still oozing gratitude for their presence. Oblivious to their appearance and demeanor.

All of Christian's clothes are still in his suitcase. It looks as if, only a woman stays there.

I'm grateful I put our passports in the safe when I did. Lord, what if I left them on the desk and they found them? They would have known I was still in the country somewhere.

I shut my eyes and pray, 'Lord, don't let her tell them we're here.' We move to Jeff's main door that opens to the hall and I look out the peephole.

"Yeah, yes. I'm alone." She says unconsciously, glancing at Jeff's door.

Knowing her, it's revenge to ensure we don't get rescued with her.

"Americana?" says the Officer coming out of my room.

She is so self-centered she doesn't see their work boots and that their uniforms don't fit. It looks as if they just threw a police shirt over their civilian clothes. A small tattoo on the back of their hands, along with their pockets bulging from the loot they probably gained from abandoned rooms.

"Yes, I am American… um… did the hotel or my husband send you?" she asks, looking uncomfortable now.

She backs away from them down the hall.

"Por'Favor, come with me." he puts one hand on his holstered gun.

"No. I'm sorry," she says trying to make light of the moment, "I just remembered, my husband said he would meet me in the lobby." She looks at her watch. "I'll just go meet him."

"He's downstairs." Says the scarred officer. "Really. I don't think so."

She turns and runs past Jeff's door down the hall toward the stairwell. My heart is racing, and I put my hand on the door to brace myself. They are ambling behind her, laughing. Behind her, two more armed men dressed as officers block her exit. They trap her.

I pray. She needs a miracle, but if she turns to our door, she will give us away.

"No, no, please. I have children… I have money. What do you want!" she pleads while backing away from them.

Then two men grab her from behind. The one that knocked on the door is wearing a surgical glove. He takes a damp cloth from his pocket.

"Open the door! Help me! Please..." she yells, reaching for Jeff's door."

I can't watch it anymore. I think I'm having a panic attack. My heart is racing, I'm sweating and I can't breathe. I stagger toward the sofa. Jeff goes to the peep-hole.

I hear bumps and kicks on the door. Her cries become muffled. The cloth is over her nose and mouth by now. Then... silence.

Jeff backs away from the door, taking one soft step backward. He turns to me and puts his finger over his lips again, then points at the door. The Officer must have wondered if anyone is in here.

The nob turns. Thank God it's locked. The fake Officer jerks it hard. Jeff takes one finger and gently pushes the metal catch over the stopper, then backs away from the door further.

I can't breathe. My chest is heaving and I open my mouth wide to get as much air as possible without making a sound. I shut my eyes and tilt my head back. Both my hands are on my heart. It's pounding through my fingers.

"Abierta La Puerta! Open the door!" One Officer yells from the connecting door.

We are cornered. One fake officer at the main door and the other at the connecting door. I feel a tear fall from my eye. All I can do is pray. It's just a matter of time.

CAPTURED

CHAPTER TWO

Caleb Promise
Three Weeks Ago

For the first time in years, I slept. And I slept soundly. I dreamed and didn't control a thing in my dream. I rested in the dream and watched like a spectator. Like a regular person.

No nightmares. Not one. I awoke, rested. Haven't rested in so long. This bed soft as a cloud. After what I just went through, I guess it would only make sense that I was dead. But I'm not. I don't know how Jason managed this, but I have to admit it is much better than going back to the cheap extended stay hotel in Manhattan. These sheets don't scratch. It seems weird, but I want to know what kind they are.

"Egyptian cotton 1500 thread count,"

I never read the label on the sheets I used to sleep on. Funny, what sticks with you. There is a must in my old roach-ridden dwelling. It got in my clothes. This smells new. Everything is new. I run my hand through my cut hair. Still not used to it being this length. I turn to the right, toward the softly glowing sheer curtains on the balcony's closed French doors.

It's real. Biarritz. The water, just beyond my balcony. The dresser, heavy craftsman. Every detail screams money, even to the smallest silver dresser tray with manicure set beside a silver comb and brush. I don't think I'll ever touch that. Only ever used a five-dollar plastic brush from a pharmacy.

The dresser draws are empty. All I have is one pair of jeans, a shirt, and my brown waist-length leather jacket, with leather ankle height boots; even those, Wallie gave me as replacements for mine destroyed in that last fiasco. How he got *my* leather jacket, I'll never ask.

Easy, I guess, for the heir of a billionaire. The ceiling fan above the bed matches the decor perfectly. Wallie didn't miss a trick. What is that? Something is crackling.

I sit up and scoot back, leaning against the headboard. The fireplace is lit. Fresh logs. It's clean. Something is comforting about the sound of the crackling logs. Looks like it's the first time it's ever been lit. It wasn't lit last night. Didn't even hear anyone come in. They lay a bathrobe across the seat in front of the fire, toasty warm by now.

It's not freezing. Then again, my inner thermostat is off. The last few years broke it. My concept of cold is far more extreme than most. New York did that to me.

"Sir. Caleb. Are you awake?" a voice says.

I look around the room. No one. I hear Wallie laughing.

"Video-com. The tablet on your nightstand. I can't

see or hear you unless you press talk."

Already.   I'm getting soft. I pick up the tablet and press talk.

"Wallie, this is-"   I say.

"-come to breakfast.   I'd send it up, but I want you to see something."

"Wallie-"

"-tell me when you see me.   Come on.   The breakfast-room."

He disconnects. He looks happy. Thrilled. Then again, there's only one day since I knew him he didn't look happy.   The day I watched his limousine pull out of the orphanage.

"The breakfast-room?"

Surrounded by all of this is wonderful, but I can't help but be uneasy. All of this is great, but it isn't mine. None of it. I know what Wallie said, but a man earns what a man gets. If a man doesn't work, a man doesn't eat. That's what I was taught.

I didn't earn this. Unsettled. That's the word I'm looking for. Unsettled. How do I tell him I have to go?   I'll figure it out later.

I put the tablet down and go into the equally impressive connecting lavatory.

From extravagant to more extravagant. The bathroom has a shower and a separate bathtub. Where I come from, it's an either-or thing. After a hot shower, I am refreshed. I dress and even put some aftershave on.

Even at my height, I feel small. Everything in this house dwarfs a man. Standing at the top of the main stairwell, its grandeur emanates standing on the top of the world.

Vaulted arched ceilings with ornate arched moldings soar over the massive wide staircase with wrought iron banisters. I can't even imagine how costly these paintings are.

In the corner of my eye, a slight movement. A lady dressed in black and white with her hair in a tight bun. She's dusting in the corner and a well-dressed woman holding a large ledger walks silently across the room in soft-bottom shoes. She puts her hand on the doorknob of a wooden door, sees me, and pauses.

"May I help you?" she asks.

I descend the steps, walking toward her. Every word echos like a museum.

"I'm-" I begin.

"-I know who you are, Mr. Promise. Good afternoon. How may I help you?"

Her words are polite, her mannerisms, curt. She's saying all the right words, but her tone lets her character escape. I guess she isn't used to people sleeping into the afternoon around here. Her emphasis on that word reflects her disdain.

I wonder if she stands silently at the foot of Wallies' bed every morning, scaring the life out of him when he opens his eyes. No, she seems like the type to walk in, rip the curtains open and throw open the windows, letting blasts of chilly air wake you.

She doesn't like me, or does she just not like me, here? Now, I want to stay to find out.

"The breakfast-room?" I ask.

She looks me up and down. But why? I'm clean. Next, she'll pull out a ruler and crack me on the knuckles.

I'm wearing *my* clothes. All of them. Boots, jacket and all.

"Will you be going out?"

Not even her question sounds like a question.

"No," I say flatly.

"Shall Marisol take your outer coat, Sir? Caleb?" She asks sliding her eyes to the housekeeper dusting in the corner who straightens.

"I'm fine. Thank you."

She doesn't like that one. She rolls her eyes in a strange, sophisticated way by looking straight up at the ceiling. All she's missing is her head spinning completely around.

"Down that corridor, through the French doors to the right. Mr. Davenport is expecting you. Will you be expecting company?"

"No," I answer.

"Good."

I turn, to look down the corridor, and turn back to say thank you but the large wooden door she was entering, close behind her then stop, leaving a three-inch opening. Her eyes locked on me until I am out of her view. The maid in the corner smiles at me and continues dusting.

I'm not nosy, but he caught my eye. A man sitting in the open entryway dressed in a suit, looking hopeful. His knees together and feet flat on the floor, awkwardly holding his briefcase upright in his lap. He looks like he's waiting for his turn in the dentist's chair, trying to not let his back touch the antique chair. The corners of his eyes turn upward, smiles at me.

It's obvious. He thinks I'm Wallie so must be new here. He's nervous for no reason. Wallie's the nicest person he'll ever meet.

I start down the corridor. A few more steps and an open door into my right reveals another person in an office. Wallie's office, I'm guessing by the décor.

He's different. His eyes are small and I can't make out their color. In, his late sixties and he has been here before. Suited in a three-piece with immaculate shoes. He reeks of aftershave and his nails shine. Standing on the opposite side of an enormous desk, he is reading through a file.

He looks at me, doesn't smile, or gesture a hello, then

looks at his watch and continues thumbing through the file as if I were not standing there. Interesting. Wallie is more alone here than I thought.

I have never even heard of a breakfast room. In my family, we called it a kitchen. I don't see a kitchen. I don't even smell food. A wall of glass from ceiling to floor shows a sun-room with a circular table covered by a white tablecloth, flowers in the center, set for three. Wallie sits, legs crossed, reading a floppy paper newspaper.

Against the wall, a long table with chafing dishes with small warming burners beneath them and a server standing in a gray serving uniform with white gloves. One hand with the other, he is standing, waiting. Large glass flasks of three different juices and hot coffee are to his left.

He's my age, in his mid-twenties, and he's just about my height. I am taller by a foot or so. His eyes, dark brown. His hair, loaded with hair gel, slicked straight back. I pull the door by an invisible silver vertical bar and it slides silently aside.

"For a moment, I thought I would need to send Mrs. Bird after you," Wallie says, folding his paper.

I sit across from him with our seats angled so we both have a view overlooking the grounds. A full-length swimming pool with immaculately trimmed hedges surrounding a garden area in the distance.

Wallie is as I remember him. He still has that shine in his eye. He always looks excited to be alive. I used to call him 'hand-ball'. We used to play hand-ball at the orphanage.

In New York, kids, even adults, played hand-ball against

a large cement wall.   The ball was about the size of a palm with hard outer rubber, and they bounce like crazy.

Wal bounced back from things so fast, I called him 'hand-ball'.   Only in private.   No one ever heard me say that.   He is unlike me, hold everything far too long. Sometimes, I wish I held that quality.

His hair is even and tapered at the ends. Slicked back with gel, it's shining.   I don't want to shine.

"Is that her name? I don't think she likes me."

"So, you've met my surrogate mother."   He laughs. "She treats everyone the same.   With contempt.   How did you sleep?"

"Better than I have in years." I sit back in the seat. "Wallie, I wanted to talk to you about-"

"-five acres.   My father bought it as a second home because my mother loved the sea.   Now, it's me.   Just me. I was excited when Jason called me."

Wallie is smart.   He's smart enough to know that I won't stay anywhere I feel I'm not wanted and I won't stay where I feel I'm not needed.   He's giving me both, in one offer.   Clever.

"What can I give you that Mrs. Bird, or that guy in the office or even your new server over there can't give you?"

"Precisely that.   You have been here less than twenty-four hours and already you're doing your 'thing'."

"What thing, Wallie. I have done nothing. Look, you don't have to pat me on the back for me to-"

"I'm not. I'm not patting you, rest assure. You see things, Caleb. You miss little and that's what I need here. Eyes. Honest eyes." He sips orange juice with pulp in it from a tall tubular glass. "For example, what makes you think my server is new?" Wallie squints, smiling.

His eyes go over the server from head to toe, looking for clues. I look straight at Wallie.

"Most obviously, his shoes. Brand new."

"He could have just needed a fresh pair."

"They are too big. If you employed him long, and knowing you, you pay well, he would have been able to afford a pair that fit. Look at where he is standing."

Wallie looks.

"So what? He's standing in front of the table."

"Experienced servers stand to the side of the table allowing the person to walk up and look at what's inside without having to ask him to move. Most of all, his eyes. He's unsure of himself. His heart rate is elevated and so is his breathing. He's nervous. I guess that he didn't just take this job for the money. There is something else." I pause.

"What else?"

"Access."

"To what?"

"Not what, whom. You. He will probably ask you for a personal loan, larger than anything he would get as a server. Thus, his purpose for the job. Knowing you, you would give it to him and he knows that. He'll read you as soft and end up stealing from you." I say, watching Wallie tip his head toward me.

"You're incredible. I know you possess deduction, however, Caleb, that is a little far-fetched."

I stand, go to the table with the food, and the server does an uncertain sidestep in both directions, trying to decide how to not block my path. In doing this, he knocks over a serving spoon and fiddles in a serving draw for another.
I say something to him and he smiles. I tell him what I want to eat and return to the table.

"What was that?"   asks Wallie confused.

"Breakfast," I say.

The server approaches the table and puts down a square white plate from my left with my selections on it. I lift my look to Wallie, who drops his eyes and smiles. He knows proper serving etiquette is that you serve from the right and clear from the left.

"Thank you..." I say to the server.

"You were saying, you'll be away for three months?" I say to Wallie as I salt my eggs.

Puzzled, Wallie thinks as I knew he would, and follows suit.

"Yes. Three glorious months in the London property. Will you come?"

"Nope. You still leaving after breakfast?" I ask.

"Yes. The car is waiting." Says Wallie looking at his watch.

We note the continence of the server. It has fallen. He's red in the face and fussing with things on the table that need not be touched.

"Are you all right?" Wallie asks the server.

"Well, Sir. Since you've asked, I was hoping to speak with... well, ask... you something. It can wait."

This tastes good. I avoid Wallies' eyes. He has fallen serious. This is different. A side of him I've ever seen.

"Please, ask." Says Wallie leaning back in his chair.

"Well, I am grateful to work for you but I need-"

I stand and return to the food table.   The server follows me.

"-No, no stay."   I say ushering him back to Wallie.

I lag at the table, giving them time to talk. When I returned to the table, the server goes back to the serving table and resumed his stance.   Wallie is pensive.   Leaned forward, elbows on the table and his fingers forming a triangle with its peak resting on the tip of his nose.

"I gave it to him and let him go." Says Wallie.

I put my fork down, wipe my mouth with my napkin and hold it bunched up in my hand, chewing the best sausage I ever tasted.   I lean in toward him.

"You fired him?"   I say surprised.

"You were right about the former, so likely, correct about the latter.   Don't worry, you gave me the perfect justifiable reason. My extended trip to London."   He exhales.   "I am used to being looked at as an opportunity rather than a person. It comes along with the territory of being wealthy. People don't see 'you' they see what they can get from you. Caleb, I don't think you appreciate my position." He says biting a toast.

His vocabulary and way of speaking was always better than mine. I guess he got his money worth from all those tutors.

"Explain," I say watching him sip some coffee from

a small white coffee cup.

"A substantial amount of responsibility rests on my shoulders and I must have the right people around me to make the right decisions.   There are few people I can trust.   These people, all of them, worked with my father. He hand-picked them and they were loyal to him.   I'm uncertain that loyalty transferred to me.

I understand the logistics of this lifestyle, but you catch what I miss.   In my position, I must see everything. I'm not asking you to stay here as just a benefit for you, but a tremendous burden lifting for me.   I'm tired, Caleb."

"Shut up."

"I'm serious."

"You're too young to be tired."

"I'm tired of trying to do all of this alone.   I'm thrown advice, most of which I can deduce mathematically and pragmatically, however the rest evades me.   You learn that if you show them where your weakness is, they will exploit it.   They will dig in like ravenous dogs and go in for the kill.

My father's company board of directors of which I hold the majority share.   There are some, well, most of them, want to taint my reputation to have me voted out as incapable.   I've made mistakes even with access to my father's diaries and logs."

"Logs?"

"He left, shall I say, a road map of advice. The best he could get overtime. But even so, I need *my* team. My confidants. An inner circle I can trust. I want to start with you. It will be you. And we selected the rest.

I see a new direction I intend to head in and I can't have people who may undermine me in the planning. No one will be over you, but me. Your word will be my word. Do you accept?"

Who is this person? He's not throwing pomegranates and getting splinters in his butt from sliding down the banister. This Wallie is a grown thinking man.

Now, I feel as if I were being very self-centered and selfish. His need is my need. That's the pact we made beneath the moonlit sky with the flames of our funeral clothes burning in the pit at our feet when we were sixteen still stands. With his face serious, I see more in him. I see his heart. He wants to do this right. He's dedicated. Loyal.

"I accept."

His nervous expression turns to a smile. He sits back and drops his napkin on his plate.

"Then, I have something to show you."

"What is this?" I ask as we descend into the basement. We stand in front of an enormous cement door with no doorknob.

"My vision. The Think Tank." Says Wallie placing his face in front of what looks like a scratch on the cement wall beside the door.

A beam expands over his face from forehead to chin. Then the cement door slides to the right. The wall slides to the right. It's a hidden door.

The room is massive. It is the entire size of the house. To the left, a sitting area, to the right, a glass-enclosed conference size table with a monitor in the rear, a massive gym with every piece of equipment you can think of.

The conference area is a think tank with gadgets, guns, explosives, body armor and digital floating maps of the world.

"Our Think-Tank. Originally, it was my gym. Then, Jason called me and I had that added." He points to a large glass-top table at stand-up height with a rotating hologram globe hovering over it.

I look at him and he must see that I am confused because he explains before I can think of a good question. The door's seal behind us.

"It is a bunker. It's bomb proof and we build the entire house like a bunker. The depth of the window casements are steel and lead-lined-plates that will seal them off in the event of an emergency. You can trigger it or it will automatically engage if the house is physically impacted with, let us say, a bullet."

"Lead-lined? What are you prepared for, a nuclear bomb?" I chuckle.

Wallie doesn't smile at all.

"Yes. It is a verified nuclear bunker. If it happens, the house lowers." He pops a piece of candy from a dish in his mouth.

"The house."

"Yes."

"Lowers?"

"Lowers. Into the ground and seals its self."

"What do you mean, the house lowers?" I ask.

"Dad had the house built on a lift foundation. In the event of a bombing, or God forbid, nuclear attack, the entire house will descend into the ground and seal itself beneath nuclear-proof plates. The ventilation system and plumbing become self-sufficient and detaches the house from the grid.

It will run on its own. The windows in the gym and sitting area are bulletproofed and, with the touch of a button, ten-inch cement walls will rise and seal the facility from the outside airtight. Over there," he points to a kitchen area with hidden cabinetry, "which is enough food for five people to survive for five years. It has with every modern comfort. But just about everything in the room has an alternate use.

The fireplace, for example, is indeed a fireplace but has a self-destruct feature enabling it to blow fire and engulf the facility destroying everything. Let's hope it's never necessary. We are safer than the President of the United

States. " He flicks something off his sleeve.

"Wallie. You need a vacation."

"I'm serious, Caleb.   On this side of the fence, you can't even breathe like everyone else. I know things about this world that most people don't. With wealth, comes power. With power comes enemies."

"What are you planning?" I ask, sitting on the sofa.

"To make an actual difference."
He sits. "When my mother died, I was helpless. My father died, I was helpless. A power took them greater than money. My vision, to empower the helpless. Financing the vision is not an issue.

I'm not talking about paying off mortgages or scholarships for college, I'm already doing that. I'm talking about tipping the scale. You have access to leaders. What can't we achieve?"

The last mission is coming back to haunt me already.   I thought all that was over with.   Something in his words sparks inside of me. I can do it. It is workable, but part of me wants to be a regular man. Go to the local store and get some jeans and an ice cream kind of man.

I stand and drift through the room. Attention to detail is everywhere. His eyes flicker and if I'm honest, I enjoyed seeing the last mission solved.   Well, sort of solved. The master-mind, the one who funded the BST-10 Project and ordered my parents' murder, is still out there. I want him. This endeavor gives me the means and a partner. Yet, I feel targeted.

"So, you chose me because of my connection to the leaders?" I ask Wallie.

"No. I am not the server."

"Really."

"Caleb, your connections aren't difficult to gain. What is difficult to gain is passion? You and I sat helpless in that orphanage because someone took something from you and disease took something from me. People don't gain a passion for justice until something unjust happens to them. Passion is paramount in something of this magnitude.

I want what my father worked for all his life to benefit far more than just filling a trust fund. I have no children, no heirs..." he turns away from me, glancing out the window, "... and I need to leave… something."

There is something to that. I can feel it, but now is not the time to address it. My heart is thumping in my chest. I claim my cause. I will bring my parent's murderer to justice. People like that don't stop unless a greater or equal force stops them.

"Whatever you need me to do, I'm in." I hold my hand out to him.

He bypasses my hand and hugs me and I feel the weight of the world come off of his shoulders, but has it come onto mine? He steps back in typical Wallie-form and hits me in the arm. The old-Wallie the adventurer's smile returns.

"Your trainer will be here at seven in the morning." He says walking away backward smiling.

My smile drops.   Why the urgency?

"Why so early? Can't we make it at ten?"   I ask, walking behind him.

"Weapons specialist comes at ten."

"You knew I'd say yes," I say crossing my arms.

"No. But I plan for the best and solve the worst."

I can't help but shake my head, watching him walk to the door.

"Caleb. You will get a telephone call. Answer it. They will ask for a meeting. Take it."

"Why should I?"

"Obey your elders."   He runs out of the room.

I catch up to him as before and smack him in the back of the head, cut him off and run up the steps. Him running right behind me like old times and this is beginning to feel like home.

CAPTURED

CHAPTER THREE

Jason Jones

I pop the pill in my mouth and swallow it with water from the small paper cup. I never thought I'd be taking pills at forty-eight. My back has been bothering me all night. I barely slept. I hope no one heard my grunt as I bent for the cup at the water cooler. This is the wolf's den. They can smell blood and weakness.

I learned early to hide any aches and injuries. Before I know it, they will whisper word of my incapability to execute my job all over the White House.

In times past, standing in a White House hall waiting would have been easy. This will be a lonely birthday. I don't care what the number says; I feel ten years older. This job can easily do that.

The meeting ended ten minutes ago. The over-sized double doors are open. A routine update insignificant in itself, however, the attendance of Martin Worthly's assistant in the hall nervously scribbling beside the General's assistant who is scrolling through his social network account, has my eyebrows up.

Martin is the Director of the United States Passport and

Travel Division. Why would he be in this meeting?

I press my back against the cool wall and brace both feet flat on the floor when everyone in the hall stops. One by one head turn toward a large television screen down the hall. This is where it counts to pay attention.

I push my glasses up on my face with a flick and focus on the screen, slightly blocked by people blankly drifting toward it. I take a glance into the office at those seated around the table. The President looks at his watch and stands to leave the meeting, followed by everyone at the table when the Secretary of Defense's Personal Assistant rushes into the room and whispers in his ear.

A flat expression and he shares the news with those at the table. They sit. Someone in their room turns on the large wall-mounted television and they watch, somewhat unsurprised, at the billowing black smoke and flames seeping out of the roof.

The assistant closes the doors upon exiting the room. Someone turns up the television down the hall.

"They confirmed it. The footage is real. There has been an explosion at the United States Embassy in Mexico. Details are still unknown. Casualties unknown, if any. We will keep you posted as we get further information.

This has just elevated the tensions between the already stressed relationship between the United States and Mexico." Says the newscaster.

This completely changes the nature of my visit to Director White. So I stand here, waiting. After my third drink of water, I crumble the thin paper cone-cup and toss it at the small garbage receptacle beside the cooler. I miss. I bend to pick it up, and the doors finally open.

"Director White, Jason Jones was just here to see you." Says the receptionist seated outside the office doors. She does not see me picking up the paper cup behind the desk.

"Great. What's next? The plague?" says Dir. White.

I stand. They both look at me. The receptionist blushes with embarrassment. Director white doesn't. She tilts her head, exposing her long neck, and smiles sarcastically. She's turned into a twisted bird. Maybe I should offer her a pill.

"Only if you are lucky," I reply.

She draws her folder to her chest, holding it tightly, rolls her eyes at me and strides up the hall. She's different. She is confident. She's wearing a power-play suit. Strong ridges with high pumps. A splash of red in her blouse matching her red matte lipstick. She looks better with brown hair. She must have lightened it.

My wife laughs at me. Well, used to laugh at me. She would say, most men look at women for the pleasure of it, but you look at them like a scientist dissecting a specimen. Trying to find the root of its death for the mere fun of it. I can't help it.

At least Director White doesn't drown herself in perfume like most women. I know one thing; she doesn't want me to see the file pressed to her chest. I will follow her to her office. She has to put it down sometime.

"What do you need, Jason? The world is raging, you know."

She walks quick. Another negative to feeling my age. Every step sends a shooting pain into my back. I can credit this injury to a mission I took in my thirties. Young, zealous, and no match for the man I tackled. My ego got the best of me then, as it often does now. The difference is, I have learned to tackle them with words. Keeping up with her and breathing is becoming difficult.

"Not important compared to what's happening now. What's the status?"

"Wait for the report. It will get to your department as always."

"True, but by that time it is old news."

"I hate to tell you wasted your trip here. If you were supposed to know what was going on in that room, they would have invited you in."

"You know as well as I do, that tension in that region-"

"Shh!" she stops walking.

After a quick flick of my finger on the bridge of my glasses, I lower my voice but continue. "Tensions in that region right have been escalating unusually if you know what I mean. I know a move is inevitable. The President is up for re-election. I won't shut my eyes, White."

"My office. This will be a long day." Dir. White says rolling her eyes.

She takes a few more steps then pulls off her shoes, shoves them in my chest and keeps walking. She has become more comfortable with herself. Strange, her shoes don't even stink. I feel like throwing them at her. But I need her, well, I need her information, that is.

It smells like a woman in here. I drop the shoes on the floor as soon as I step in. The office looks the same. The furniture, the paint, the neutral carpet, yet there is something different. She has the most uncomfortable chairs. I'll stand.

She puts the file down on the desk face-down, removes her jacket and hangs it on the coat rack, slips on her 'office flats' and sits behind her desk and reaches for her coffee carafe taking a drink.

"All hate aside, how have you been, Jason?"

Pictures. That's what's different. A window into her personal life, but all the pictures face her. I reach for one of the frames.

"Don't touch." She slaps the top of my hand.

"With the disappearances of an unprecedented number of Americans in that region in the last week, now this? It doesn't make sense unless they have a death-wish. Amid the President's re-election campaign at that? They know we must answer back. Something doesn't feel right."

She stops mid-sip. She puts down her cup and avoids looking at me. Now I'm concerned.

"You will want to sit for this." She says.

"I'm listening," I say sitting. "The fact that your willing to tell me, makes me think I will need a drink after this meeting."

"Jason, it's no secret we clash heads, but I know what you are capable of. I know your connections. Why do you think Martin was in the meeting? I know you didn't miss that."

We have to play this game for the sake of her deniability. If I guess it, she can say she never 'told' me.

"My guess, have what looks like a political issue needing an international eye-view. Martin eats and breathes American abduction tactical negotiations. I'm thinking the President needed an update… a specific update. A verbal, non-written update." I feel my eyes squint as they search her face, the thoughts pouring out of my mouth. "But, we don't negotiate with terrorists who kidnap Americans. That's policy." I flick my glasses at the bridge of the nose.

"That is policy. But that depends on who is missing, unfortunately. A very important person has gone missing in Mexico."

"Many people, Americans, have gone missing in Mexico in the last few weeks.   It's chaos."

"Who is it, White?"   I stand.

She picks up a heavy pen, rips a page from her notepad to leave no chance of an imprint, scribbles quickly and slides it across the desk to me.

"Christian Bleu." I read.

"Hmm," I say.

She nods, lights her scented candle and holds the paper over the flame.   Designs military grade bunkers and panic rooms for us and the one percent of our population that try their best to remain unknown. The mega-rich.

"I see you've heard of him."   She rubs her two fingers across her temple as if wiping off a headache.

"By word of mouth, of course.   He doesn't advertise."

"He doesn't need to. From what I understand, his clientele prefer his discretionary approach. They like his 'quiet' presence."   She focuses her eyes on the Presidential seal on the file. I understand why.

She laces her red fingertips. "The importance of this is that he himself has a bunker he designed containing a map of the locations of his clientele's bunkers and their security parameters with emergency entry codes. It is a back-up measure. No one knows where it is except-"

"-Him. He is probably being tortured for the location of his bunker." I say.

"For this to have happened, someone knew where and when he was going, where he'd be staying. Had to be someone close." She sips her coffee.

"No, Someone like him tells no one his itinerary. Hence the purpose of Martin in the meeting. My guess is, he always handles his travel plans personally. Okay."
I'm pacing. I think. My feet are moving. I flick my glasses. I'm not speaking to her. I'm thinking aloud for myself. She is here. I continue.

"The registry. Knowing him, he registered his trip like any wise American and this man is wise. He's alive. He must be. No ransom?"

"No.," she says.

"No. How long has he been missing?"

"Two days."

"There won't be one because what they want is more important than money. Someone who targets a person like him wants power, not money. Two questions. Question, why did he choose Mexico? With all his money he could have gone anywhere... wait, sentiment.
It must have been sentiment. It defies logic and someone who designs secure bunkers; he secures. What

would make a man like him defy logic? Love. My guess is he was not alone. Dear God, wife?" I look up at Dir. White and her pensive eyes confirm my deduction. "She must still be there or it would have been all over the news." I exhale. "Question, what are we doing about it? Every politician, world leader and billionaire he worked for will figure this out. And it won't take them long. As soon as this hits the news, we're screwed."

She's staring at me. Just holding her coffee, staring at me.

"Close your mouth," I say, sitting down in the uncomfortable chair opposite her.

"This is what it's like inside your head. Lord. I want out." She says putting down her cup and rolls her eyes.

"He registered his trip, didn't he? A man like him would. What happened?" I ask her.

"He did." She inhales. "We had a rat in the Bureau of Consular Affairs. This isn't the first time. He would keep an eye out for 'persons of interest' traveling and sell their itinerary to whoever was interested."

"Had. So, you have him. How long has that been going on?"

Dir. White smooths her hair back, leans back in her chair and exhales.

"Two years." She says shaking her head.

My mind is running through the list of American abductions that occurred during that time. Now it makes sense. I stand in front of the desk. The chair is terrible. My back feels best when I'm upright.

"Yes. You were right about everything you said. We questioned family and friends. A sister-in-law, a brother, but no one else knew about his plans. Not even his business partner."

I walk around to her side of the desk and sit on the edge, fold my arms facing her.

"Who was the buyer?" I mouth to her with my back intentionally to the hidden camera on her bookshelf.

She shakes her head 'no' meaning they don't know yet.

"Anyway, it's being handled. Are you going to Robert's birthday party?" she asks.

"Thought about it. Where is it?" I ask, following her lead.

"Here's the address. Bring a gift, Jason." She rips a page off of her notepad and scribbles. She puts the pen down on the desk with a slight thump and slides the paper to me.

"We believe that the other disappearances may have been to mask one this his. The President and many other people of, let's just say, stature, would have an interest in seeing him returned safely, or dead. Either. Preferably the former. Our intervention in getting this person back must executed quietly."

"How quietly?" I ask, shifting my weight, I lean on the desk. I need her to be specific. No gray areas. She discreetly glances at the paper in my hand.

"C.P. vital." It reads.

She can't say his name. After the last mission, everyone knows his name. This is an off-the-table ask. I fold the paper and push it in my breast pocket.

The President can't be seen to break policy. C. P. Is Caleb Promise. She wants me to send Caleb into hostile territory where American's are being kidnapped and killed because of a sudden rise in criminal activity in Mexico to find Christian Bleu. The risks are all Caleb's. If he's caught by the officials, we both must deny knowledge of him and any involvement. If he's caught by rebels, he is on his own.

"Why not one of ours? A team?"

"The President can't have so much as a dusty halo during this re-election, and the White House is leaking like a broken fountain right now. It would raise too many questions on too many levels."

I fold the paper and slip it into my trouser pocket.

"There are two positions presented here. One, the campaign and public opinion.   President is in the middle of his re-election campaign and the last thing he wants to risk sacrificing is the Hispanic and minority vote.

However, two, the retrieval of *him* at all costs. We need a less obvious solution to this problem that offers the greatest deniability."

"If he had to choose, would he lose the campaign to get him back?" I need to know the true value of what this man knows.

"Yes." She says flatly.

I feel that drop again. The one in the pit of my stomach when I first realized Caleb surfaced during the last mission. To understand the depth of millions of dollars and years of work required for a presidential campaign, that he would divest from that goal is terrifying. Desperate men are dangerous men.

"The wife?" I ask.

"Still in Mexico. She contacted the U. S. Embassy there. Mr. Hannorai Douglas, one agent, was smart enough to look up her husband's name and contacted us immediately. Jason, we can't bring her home yet... for obvious reasons."

"Press."

"Exactly. She will talk. That's her husband. We can't quash it. It was their twenty-fifth wedding anniversary. They went there for their first honeymoon. Sentiment."

"The longer you leave her there, you increase her

chance of being taken and used as leverage against him. You know that don't you."

"If they wanted to, they would have taken them together. This is key Jason, she can't come home... not yet." Says Dir. White.

I rise and walk to the door. Pull out my right hand and open the door.

"The fact we just spent the last ten minutes talking about a missing man when an embassy is still smoking, tells me I don't have time to waste."

"Do you think he'll do it?"

I shrug. I hate myself for having to ask him. But there is a bigger picture here. One Caleb doesn't even know. During the last mission, Gretchen gave us nothing. After hours of interrogation, that nut didn't crack. So, the mystery player, the mastermind of the last plot, he or she is still out there. The person responsible for murdering his parents is still out there.

That's me, the bearer of bad news. I will never get used to this role. I pop a small white pill in my mouth.

"Why not, it's a dream job?" I look down at her shoes near the door and kick them.

She sits straight up as if I kicked her dog or something.

"Idiot." She says turning to her computer.

I let the door close behind me, stepping into the hall still buzzing with people talking about the embassy explosion.

CHAPTER FOUR

I process this in my hotel room. There are fewer ears and eyes. Strangely, I prefer Washington D.C. now. The hard winter storm is over, and signs of spring are slipping in. A bud here, a green leaf there. Perfect. Cool and comfortable.

Finally, I can show my pain. I lean over putting one hand on the bed and rest the other on the small of my back. My bag is still on the foot of the bed.

I fish around in it and my hand finds her photo. I know it's better for me to not carry it, but I can't help it. She's my only weakness. My vulnerable spot. She makes me feel alive because she's my tie to the real world. A world that fades when I'm engulfed in a case. The world that gets coffee in shops with little round tables and laughs at short snappy jokes. She's the lifeline that pulls me back and makes me dance and watch silly movies while eating popcorn. I did things with her that I normally would never try.

We visited the Grand Canyon and I sure never would have done that without her. I got sunburned, and she got some great photos for our albums. She took pictures of everything. Even things that looked like they weren't worth photographing.

Somehow, she finds value in insignificant things. It rubbed off on me and now, I get some of my most valuable information from things I originally thought were insignificant. She's teaching me, even in her absence. Sometimes it feels like I'm mourning her. I'm hoping that her heart hasn't drifted away. I'm hoping it stayed true to me through all of this empty time.

My love for her isn't going anywhere, but her, that long flowing light brown locks and deep true eyes. Who wouldn't fall in love with that?

She turned heads when she walked into places without even realizing it. What else could I do but be glad to be the one with her? We tried for children; the doctor said she could never have them so we talked about adoption but then, this case emerged.

I'm no fighter or muscle man. Well, at one time, but not now. Time has a cruel effect on some, and I'm just not the gym type. It makes me feel funny to go sweat on purpose.

She said it would be good for me if I cut loose and went for a run. When I get her back, we'll run. And run far.

I need to focus. This is the hardest mission I think I have to embark on because I have to sacrifice Caleb to get her back.

He'll probably hate me. Caleb is straightforward, and that's what he appreciates. Liars look for lies and the honest seek honesty in people. Sometimes they assume it's there, even though it's not. He'll probably think I deceived him but I didn't, well not directly.

He knows I'm an agent first, then a friend. My objective

is the same as it was after that last mission, to find the true head funding the Beaston. Gretchen vanished, so Caleb is my only pipeline into information. Steve Harvard said she 'got away' after his wife finished with her. That translates to, 'she's in a shallow ditch or already cremated with her ashes scattered in the ocean.'

I straighten and sit in the upright chair at the desk beneath the window. It's a sunny room, and the bed is great, but I don't believe in sitting on beds. They are for sleeping. Using things for what they were made for, that's my motto.

I use spies for information, and that's what I use them for. Even when they don't know they are spying.

I miss Sam. I wish she was what I thought she was. I watched her being handcuffed and taken right out of her office in Langley. A warning to other hidden double-agents who were undoubtedly watching.

Mostly, I miss my wife. A day doesn't go by without me thinking about us being together. I had to do it. I had to send her away for her safety. Most agents do it for the wrong reasons. Guilt for infidelity. An excuse to be free or they got lost in their character. Mine is clear and true.

I sent my love away because I was being hunted and it hurt finding out that my spy was Sam and she knew about it. I think the last mission aged me five years.

Hopefully, Caleb will understand the real reason I sent him to Wallie's. I can't delay anymore. I dial the number and video-call him.

"Hello? It's me, Jason." I say, propping the camera phone against the desk lamp.

"It's video Jason, you don't have to say your name. Good to see you!" Caleb says happily.

I don't think I've ever seen him happy. Ever. Now I feel guilty. I don't want to drag him in again. I know what freedom looks like and this is it. He's free, but not for long.

He's in a gym? I've ever seen him do anything recreational. His last few years have been all about bare basics. He's not that lanky shell. He looks good, fit.

"What are you doing?" I ask.

"Working out. For the first time in my life." Caleb says kicking a large hanging bag.

"Higher!" Yells a male voice.

"Who is that?" I ask.

"My trainer. Wave, this is Jason." Caleb turns his phone revealing the sculpted muscular man standing with both hands steadying a red punching bag. He has a bandanna tied around his head, a shirt that clings to every muscle in his six-pack and is wearing gloves with the fingers cut out.

"I don't wave." The trainer says expressionless.

Caleb laughs and throws his towel at him.

"He's always like that. I need a moment. Russ. Give me ten minutes." Caleb says and I hear a slide door shut.

"Why are you working out?" I ask.

"Same old, Jason. You always have to find the reason someone does something. You know, some people do things just because it makes them feel good."

I pause and think.

"Nope. I know nothing about that." I answer.

Caleb is looking at me and his smile lowers. He's in. He's digging into my brain. I almost hate talking to someone who does what I do. Almost. We save a lot of words because we often talk with our eyes. I would have just called him on the telephone, but I wanted to see how he was truly doing. He looks different. Very different. He is happier than I have ever seen him. Strangely, he doesn't seem surprised to hear from me.

"What's going on?" Caleb asks, looking behind him. Russ is benching the heavyweight with ease.

"We need to meet," I say.

Caleb nods at me.

"Text me when and where." He says and hangs up.

That was too easy. He didn't ask me why. My flight arrives in Biarritz, and I drive straight to our meeting location. A seaside restaurant overlooking the dock. Something calming about boats swaying on a calm sea. The problem, the sea isn't calm. The boats are tapping the dock.

I chose it because it's noisy. That won't make it easy to be overheard. Also, it's casual, like me. Sort of rough around the edges. Funny, now that I think about it, that's how I choose all of my restaurants.   Rough and loud.

"A booth by the window, please," I tell the host.

The restaurant is full.   Perfect.   The clank of silverware and chatter makes a restaurant come to life.   Simple. No tablecloths. No pretense, just wood polyurethane tables, and paper napkins.

I ordered for us.   Caleb's not late, I'm just always early. It's a habit.   I look over the place and if I get any red flags or indications it's not safe, I text "RED" to Caleb and he will stay away.

It's a code I used for my wife.   This was our routine when we went out to eat.   She got used to me preceding her.   She didn't like it, but she knew it was necessary given my line of work as a Central Intelligence Agent.

"Let me guess, you ordered already," Caleb says walking up to the table just as I got settled.

I didn't see him come in, which means he was here already. Knowing him, he was watching to see if it was safe. He is taller than I recall and a whiff of his leather jacket came to the table with him.

There is a shine to him. A lightness he didn't have living in that drab hole in New York. He slides into the booth opposite me.

"You look well," I say smiling.

I can't help it. It's good to see him. Almost like sitting down with your favorite nephew.

"You, look like someone with a lot on his mind." He says taking off his jacket, tossing it on the seat beside him.

Honesty right off the bat. I expect nothing less than that from Caleb. It's refreshing. I nod. I don't have to speak much around him. Guilt is settling deeper into my bones.

"How are things at Wallies?" I ask.

The waitress comes to the table, a tray balanced in her left hand, and serves with her right.

"Lobster bisque soup, stuffed mushrooms, artichoke dip with lime chips and two sodas. Extra napkins. Enjoy." She leaves quickly after flashing Caleb a flirtatious smile. He ignored it completely.

We both watched her walk away until we see her fake smile drop.

"Things are good." He says. "I tried to call you to thank you for setting things up with Wallie but you went dark."

"I had to. You two get along all right?"

"It is like seeing a brother.   I imagined nothing like that. I thought when the mission was over-"

"-I would send you back to New York?" I finish his sentence.

"Exactly. It was the only 'place' I had. No family," he shrugs, "just you and Wallie. How did you know to contact him?" Caleb plucks at the food.

"Actually, that's why I wanted to meet with you, Caleb. I needed to talk to you about Wallie and his father."

He put his fork down. The wind has picked up outside. The water, now choppy, slaps the sides of the boats pitching side to side. He puts his hands at his sides, chews, and swallows.
   Now, outside, it looks as if a storm is brewing.

"Where is this going?"   asks Caleb defensively.

He's bonded to Wallie. I will have to play this cautiously. I pick up a chip and dip it into the artichoke dip and chase it with a sip of soda to keep the social element of our meeting going.

"Well, some things came to light after the last mission. Caleb, we believe Wallies' father may have had something to do with the Beaston Project and possibly with our mystery mastermind behind that tattoo on the hand of the man that tried to kill me." I pause.

He needs to absorb that. I see his lowered eyes close for one long blink and he shakes his head ever so slightly side to side. I can't tell if it is because of unbelief or because of disgust.

"That's the same as saying Wallie's father had something to do with killing my parents. Is that what you want to say to me, Jason?" his face turns red.

"Calm down, Caleb. I'm just giving you the facts on some new information I got-"

"Is it new? Is it! Or did you have this intel before you sent me to Wallie's? Whatever you do, don't lie to me."

This is crucial. If I am not honest, he'll walk out that door. If I lie, he'll see it. If I tell him the truth, he will hate me. All I can see is my wife's face.

"All right. Yes, I had the information before." I slide the stuffed mushrooms in front of him. He ignores them and just looks at me. "Around the time of your father's death, William Davenport, Wallie's father, invested heavily in technology and was searching for bio-engineers."

"Could have been a coincidence." Caleb sips his drink and scans the room.

"William Davenport was thought to be doing this to find a cure for his wife's illness and dabbled in genetic modification. However, his wife died, and the project continued then, accelerated."

"Could have been to keep others from suffering the way she did." He pops a stuffed mushroom into his mouth.

"We have a record of him having close ties with the former Secretary of Defense, John Wilkes predecessor, and recruiter. He helped Davenport acquire some property... in Brazil." I pause, knowing he'll put the pieces together.

He's quiet. "I'm not saying he did it, I'm just giving you the facts, so you know what you're living with."

"Really. I'm living with it because you sent me there. Truth is, you wanted a spy. You sent me there to feed you information, didn't you? It was not out of the goodness of your heart to give me..." Caleb wipes his mouth with a napkin.

"... a new life. A friend. A place to live. Go on, say it."

"All right. No, I didn't. I didn't find Wallie out of the goodness of my heart. I fell on Wallie after finding out Davenport had a son, and that son was in the same orphanage you were in.

Yes. I sent you there to get me facts or proof, which-ever comes first. That's the cold reality of it. We have a mission to complete-"

"No. YOU have a mission to complete."

"It's not over, Caleb. Not until the mastermind caught! You're the only one positioned to do it. Tell me you don't want your parent's murderer!"

Caleb slams his hands on the table, stands and grabs his leather jacket. The restaurant falls silent, and all eyes are on us. He's imposing. It's obvious he's been working out. He's not that lanky kid I visited in the orphanage who couldn't even fill out a suit of clothing. He's muscular, and his six-foot two-inch frame lends him to tower over most men and draws more attention than I want right now.

I stand to follow him walking into the restaurant's kitchen. Dang back. Getting out of this booth is tricky. The kitchen staff let him pass but try to stop me. Great. No one will put their hands on him.

"Hey!   You can't be in here!"   says a cook to me.

"It's all right. I'm leaving."   I say holding my hands up.

Caleb bursts through the back door, and it shuts behind him. I push it open, catch the hard wind blowing into my chest and stop, seeing him standing at the edge of the grass with the water just two feet in front of him. His arms folded.

I expected him to be mad. I did. I just didn't realize how it would make me feel to see him feel betrayed by me. But I have a reason. A damn good reason. Until we find this person, I can't and won't call my wife to come back.

Until this case is closed, I'm living in an earthly hold.

"There's nothing to find. Wallie is clean. Even if his father did it, it's not Wallie. You can't hold the son responsible for what the father did."

"Wallie's father died around the same time they killed your parents. Someone kept it going. Wallie is older than you and left the orphanage before you. He inherited his father's companies… all of them. He took over. This thing kept going long after his father was dead. Someone signed the checks."

"You want me to follow the money trail. I'm no snitch, mole or spy."

"We need to know of his involvement. That's all. If it's not him, then we know he's clean and we move on. Who-ever signed it, did it?"

Caleb drops his arms, then hits his chest in anger.
"I finally have a life. Some sort of life. I would rather you sent me back to New York."

His deep blue eyes darting back and forward at mine. I put the dagger in his heart. This hurt. I see a ball of fire. That's what I'm used to seeing. This calm, happy Caleb isn't him. He's changed. Transformed into a steady man and I'm asking him to become what I became so long ago. The question is, will he?

"You once told me you didn't touch that money in the bank because you wanted to want to earn your way?

'A man doesn't work, a man doesn't eat' remember that? Make it happen right now. This is a job.

I can't let this go for a very simple reason. It's not done until it's done. That's my job. To see things to the end. Remember, when something is dead, it can't come back to hurt you. You leave these loose ends open, and you may hang on them. Your problem is you don't want to know." I say frankly.

"My problem is you are my loose end." Says Caleb.

Those words hit me straight in the chest. I need him on board at all costs.

"Caleb, we'll come back to that all right. The real reason I called is because I have a job for you."

He stops mid-stride from walking away from me.

"A man was captured in Mexico. We think he's being tortured. His wife is still there, stuck, alone."

He turns around, fists in his jacket pockets.

"I'm listening."

"Christian Bleu. He's a genius safe designer, panic-room designed for the rich and powerful. He's a good guy, taken by bad people."

"Why me? I'm no C.I.A. Agent," he asks suspiciously.

"For that very reason. You aren't C. I. A. But, you

will know how to do this right. I'll send you the details. Spin it how you must. Here," I hold out an untraceable burner phone, "call me on this."

He pauses. He doesn't want to take it. "Caleb. The Beaston Project cracked your shell. You're gifted for this like your father was. You know it.

This man has access to the secrets of the most powerful people in the world. We will go to war for his return. Hundreds may die with him and his wife, without your help.

If you take this phone, you earn your own. You won't be living off Wallie. You are independent. I'm no 'handler'. I'm just your contact. You decide. If you don't find him, war is imminent.

Caleb turns toward the water, runs his hand through his hair, then drags both hands down his clean-shaved face. He takes the phone. The back of his hand, scarred from Mission One.

He could walk away and pretend we never met. He knows I'm not vengeful. But he has a heart, and he's not the type to live off anyone for free or let the innocent die.

He steps closer to me, faces the water with his back to the restaurant. I look at his squared jaw profile as he bites his jaw.

"Don't leave through the front," Caleb says, "Director White's men are at the bar." He takes the phone and sticks it in his breast pocket and slips his fists into his jean pockets.

He turns away and starts walking down the greenbelt toward the parking lot.

"And Jason," he says not breaking stride, "tell your wife she will be home soon."

I feel a drop in my stomach. I watch him walk away with his head hung. He doesn't glance back. Not once. That's a guilt I will bear.   I have no choice.

CAPTURED

CHAPTER FIVE

Caleb Promise

That was the call Wallie said would come. I took the meeting as he advised, but nothing feels the same now. Why *does* Wallie want me here so badly? Wait, I can't let Jason get into my head. I only resisted taking the job to throw Jason off. He would have been suspicious if I said yes too soon.

I found out he's not that savior-of-an agent I thought he was. The one who sneaked into the Monastery tucked beneath a monk disguise, promising me I would find my parents' killer and do a great service to my country all at the same time. I didn't see this before.

 I want to hate him, yet I can't. I don't know why I can't. Perhaps it's because I'm done hating. I spent years hating. Carrying hate feels heavy. Years being afraid of the answers. Afraid that the worst was just around the corner. It's tiring living that way. It's absorbing, always looking, never resting and finally, finally... finally, I have rest and here he is taking it away from me. Perhaps Wallie knows Jason better than I do. He knew he would call, which means he probably already knows about the mission.

Sitting outside this majestic house in an Alfa Romeo is a dream. Cobblestone beneath the tires and I know Blake, the butler, is standing at the front door waiting to open it just for me.

Where I came from, you opened your door or stood out there till you rotted. Why would I risk all of this for Jason? For his wife? I need to think. It has been too long since I just sat and thought.

Fifteen Years Ago

Birds chirping, lots of birds and butterflies. That's what I remember being in front of our small country house, compliments of my mother's vigilant gardening skills.

Our house, far in from the street. Just half an acre backing the lake. Mom inherited it from her father when he passed away while dad was away on a mission in Afghanistan. Together, we moved what little we had from our small one-bedroom apartment with paper-thin walls.

Three-bedroom country felt like a mansion. I finally had a bedroom. That front porch went on forever, wrapping around that small ranch house.

I remember I sat in on my bike in front of the house just watching. I don't recall what caught my eye at that moment that made me stop riding with the boys, but it did, and I stopped.

I sat on my bike and stared at the house long enough to see my mother walk back and forward at least three times in the kitchen putting dinner on the table. Her mouth moving but she was alone. She was singing. Her singing filled the empty areas dad's absence left.

She set the table as if he were there. Formal. Cloth napkins, water goblets and more. No short cuts. I liked that. I don't think I ever told her, but it made me feel important. She always looked at my face when I get to the table. I hated seeing his chair empty. I want to take it away from the table, but that would have made mom feel sad. So, I left it.

I was angry that day. I was angry for the last three days. Tired of him not being here and we had to do everything and figure everything out ourselves. I had fixed the planks on the porch steps yesterday and planned to paint them the day after.

I had to work while my friends went to the spring carnival. Their dads were home and always in the work shed or riding the mowers on Saturday.

No one taught me to fix it, but mom fell bringing in groceries without me one day and cut a gash in her leg. She acted like it was nothing, but she limped for two days. It made me angry to see her limp. Things wouldn't have fallen apart if he were here.

My friends could go play while their fathers take care of the house duties. Next, I'll be cleaning out the gutters and clearing a drain in the upstairs shower. I didn't see the carnival that year.

Frankly, in retrospect, missing the carnival is not what made me angry. It was constantly missing dad. I felt abandoned. Left to figure out life while my friend's dads drove fancy cars and wore ties to work. They knew their fathers were coming home that night.

The kitchen window was open and the short curtains fluttered inward in the warm breeze. What's she doing? She stopped. She is looking right at me as if she felt me there. How?

She looked at me with concern. I smiled. I had to. She had enough on her mind. The mortgage was due in three days and dad's paycheck didn't clear yet. I found the Sunday paper on the table, open to the classifieds and a few secretarial jobs circled. I'm not angry with dad. I'm angry with his absence.

"That smells like apple pie!" I yelled to her before she got worried.

She leaned on the window, stuck her head out and the wind blew wisps of her hair in a sloppy bun, wisps of hair from her face.

"It's Wednesday.   Apple Wednesday! Ten minutes all right?"   she replied, smiling.

"Yes, Mom."

"Yes, Mommy." Joey mocked riding in circles around me.

I stuck my foot between the spokes in his front tire. The bike stopped, and he fell forward off his seat and hit that lovely bar on male bicycles. Sweet revenge. I would have heard him yelling at me, but I couldn't, not over the other guys' laughter.

We spun around in the street, talked about girls then, I saw her car coming toward us slowly.

"Caleb, I'm going to the carnival tomorrow. Meet me at the Ferris wheel?" Said Rosey.

"Good morning, ma'am,"   I say to her mother who nods and smiles.

That's the most response her mother gave, a nod and smile.   She never spoke much. Everyone knew it was because of her teeth. It was because of her mothers' teeth that Rosey and I met.   My fist met Joey's mouth for doing what Joey does best, mock. Her mother needed braces since she was a child, but her parents couldn't afford them. Rosey was self-conscious of people joking about her mother when she was in third grade.

Kids were kids and teased, but she found her backbone in fourth grade and the jokes stopped. They stopped fast. But we stayed together. We skipped rocks on the lake in the cold months, swam in the lake in the summer. We were just friends. Good friends. Best friends. People thought we were more than that but I respected Rosey and frankly, we enjoyed the candidness of our friendship. She told me things like 'if you don't stop doing... you'll never get married.' She hit harder than most guys and had honesty in her eyes. She said what she meant flat-out.

"I... I want to but... I have chores." I say, squeezing my handlebars.

"Oh, won't be done all day will you?" she asked.

She was the prettiest girl I've ever seen. It wasn't just because she could skip a rock across the lake further than I could and whistle with her fingers. She was tough and sharp.

"Might be," I said, squirming like a pup.

"Need help? I can come help. No big deal." She said.

"No. No, you go ahead. It's just house stuff. I'll try to finish fast."

"All right." She waved as the car pulled off.

It wasn't long after that day that dad came home. It was hot. Melt-the-butter hot. The hottest summer day and it hadn't rained in a while. The water level in the lake was lower than usual, and a few of the farms in the area were suffering.

I knew it was serious when the Pastor opened prayer on Sunday morning asking God to let it rain. There were lots of 'amens' after that statement. Every farmer fiddled with their feet and money in the collection plate was folded into little tiny squares.

Usually, dollar bills were folded. Not a five or a ten. Practically every bill was folded that Sunday.

Miraculously, this morning, the clouds came. He brought it with him. Beautiful big gray clouds covered the town, and the buzz was how God heard the Pastor's prayers soon followed.

Dad arrived early, and I made sure the porch was swept and freshly painted, the gutters cleaned, and I cut the grass at seven in the morning.

Mom cooked all morning and had big rollers in her hair. When the taxi pulled up, and we heard the car door slam, she came running down the steps pulling rollers out and stuck them and their pins in the drawer of the front hall table.

She looked at herself quickly in the mirror above it, straightened the vase of fresh flowers she picked from her garden and smoothed her sundress downward.

She turned around to see him standing at the screen door. It was unlocked, but he stood there on the porch and watched her.

I was in the kitchen doorway, just behind mom. I could see her then, him. I felt myself smile. That was very much a 'dad' thing to do.

My hands hung at my sides, calluses on my palms and a few nicks and cuts on my knuckles from working in the yard. I straightened my back and lifted my chin. A soldier's stance. That's what dad expected. That's what dad deserves.

He dropped his duffel bag on the patio, his eyes still locked on moms. She put her hand over her mouth, then the screech of joy escaped. He pulled the screen door open and stepped across the threshold.

I still remember the thud of his boots when he stepped into the house. Funny what you miss. Those heavy steps meant a man was in the house.

I tried to wear his shoes while he was gone. They were too big to fill. I exhaled. For the first time in months, I felt like I could breathe. I could be a kid again.

Mom ran to him, locked her arms around his neck. He lifted her off her feet and spun her like a top. I waited. I happily waited.

After a long kiss, she touched his face, and he ran his hands through those fresh curls in her hair. I missed seeing them together. They are always happiest together.

"Are you really here?" she touched his face and slid her hands down his arms.

"I'm really here." His deep voice reverberated in the room.

He looked up at me in the doorway.

"I'll warm your food." Mom disappeared into the kitchen, giving us a moment.

"Soldier," Dad says, saluting me.

I return the gesture in proper form, just as he taught me, then run into his arms. His feet didn't move. Then I ran for him. He lifted me for a second and put me back on my feet, us still in a hug.

He was going to let go, probably remembering I never liked being hugged, but this time, I held him. I held him tighter and something inside of me released.

I shut my eyes and felt my chin tremble and could feel the heat of tears forming in my eyes. He felt it and held me longer and tighter. Finally, I could let go. He was really here. I don't think I ever realized the weight that he carried. Not just as a man, but as a father and head of the house. I knew when he left that my chores would increase. That wasn't surprising, but what I didn't expect was the weight I felt from his absence. I felt him tightened his hug and heard him sniffle. What did I deprive him of, when I shrugged off his embraces in the past? I was a stupid kid.

Without him, the house felt empty. My eyes were always open when the doorbell rang. The car broke down and mom sent me to the mechanic shop. Dad told me that if you ever go to a mechanic shop, never act like you don't know what it takes to fix whatever they say is wrong. I did it. I was sweating the whole time, thinking he would figure out I was faking it.

Dad told me not to be afraid to haggle the price down because they will give you the highest price first and if you take it, you are spending more than you should. It worked. Dad was right. But with him home, I didn't have to worry about cars and gutters and salesmen. Most of all, the house felt full again. It felt right. I was a kid again.

"Well done, son.   You did well."   Dad said.

"Thanks, dad. I just missed you, that's all."   I wiped my face and smiled, assuring him.

"Mom was all right?"   he asked.

"She cried at night.   There's a quilt she liked in town but wouldn't buy it.   She needs a new pair of sneakers too, the old ones wore out but-"

"-she's saving every dime."   He said smiling.

"Yeah.   I think it scared her you wouldn't… might not come back."   I whispered, choking back the words.

Dad nodded. Swallowed.   He got it.   He stood and looked around the room slowly panning it from left to right.   He didn't miss a detail.

"Grab my bag, will you?"   he said looking at moms' built-in bookcase he made last year.

I handed it to him and he put it on the sofa.   Unzipped it and stopped, looked at me with those deep blue eyes framed by dark lashes, and smiled.
I inherited that from him.   Mom said she felt better looking into my eyes because they look just like dads and she didn't miss him quite as much.
His hair Marine short and he's muscles more defined than when he left.   He is a tall man.   I'm only fifteen but we are almost eye to eye and dad is six-foot-two inches and muscle from calves to neck.

"The house looks good.   Six months is a long time, I know.   Nice paint job on the porch too.   Good one inch cut on the grass.   You remembered." He smiled.

"Yes, Sir.   When there isn't much rain, keep it taller, keeps it from burning and dying."

"That's my boy.   This room is missing something." He glanced at above the bookcase.   "I think I have the final touch."   He took out a sheath from his long bag.

"What's that?"   I asked excitedly.

He unsnapped the leather strap over the hilt and wrapped his hand around it and pulled it from the sheath.

"This, Caleb, is a two-edged sword," Dad says smiling.   "See the blade, it's sharp on both sides, it cuts in two places."

"Dated?" I ask dad knows I'm fascinated with the history of things like this.

"1600's.   Came from daggers. It's pushed," Dad thrusts it forward into an imaginary enemy, "… like that. It is used for hacking thrusts too, but then, only one side of the blade is used.   It's more like a lunge, and the people who use them are swordsmen.   It's a two-edged sword."

"Dad, the other Sunday, the pastor was talking about two-edged swords."   I can feel my eyes widen as if fate had a hand in it being here.

"Yep, it refers the word of God to cutting like a two-edged sword, that's right. Hebrews 4, I think, can you find it?" dad asks.

He was home two minutes, and he's already got us involved in an intriguing hunt. I loved him being home. I raced to my room and found the bible.

"Here it is, Hebrews 4:12. "For the word of God is quick, and powerful, and sharper than any two-edged sword, piercing even to the dividing asunder of soul and spirit, and the joints and marrow, and is a discerner of the thoughts and intents of the heart." What does that mean?" I ask, having read it way too fast.

"It means you have to listen to bible study on Sunday. No, kidding. The word of God cuts through the toughest deepest, things in man. Gets to the core of things inside of us. Good and bad.
Caleb, one day, you and I will be like this sword." Dad holds the sword, pointing it at that imaginary bad guy again. "We will cut, me as one blade, you as the other. We will leave a mark in the minds of man."

"The mark of the two-edged sword," I said believing every word he has said though I didn't understand how, or when or why.

Most of all, I didn't understand the serious look in his eyes. His facial expression had completely changed. He was serious. Something happened. Wherever he was and whatever that mission was that he just got back from, something happened. I didn't understand it then, now. I do. Especially after that last mission.

"Lunch is ready!" mom yelled happily from the kitchen.

Dad sheathed the sword and placed it on the bookshelf. Later, after lunch, we put up brackets and mounted the sword above mom's bookshelf. It was the perfect project for a rainy day.

It rained and rained for over a week. The heavens opened on our small town, day and all night for weeks.

It must have been hysterical, we stepped back and stared at that sheathed sword above the bookcase, dad held the hammer and I held the level staring up at the sword as if we just erected the Statue of Liberty.

To us, it was. It was our first project since dad got home. I had no idea it would be our last.

CHAPTER SIX

Present Day

I'm not there anymore. I can't go any further in that memory. Beyond that point stirs anger. Besides, I don't want to keep Blake standing at the doorway any longer.

I get out of the car, a driver gets in and takes the car to the underground garage. I approach the doors, and they swing open revealing a serious, Blake.

"Good afternoon, Sir. Caleb."   Says Blake.

"Just... Caleb, Blake.   You can scrap the Sir., I told you that before."   I give him a friendly pat on the arm.

"Yes, Sir. Caleb."   Blake says closing the double doors.

I chuckle.   My voice echo in the foyer and Mrs. Bird's office to the right, perfectly positioned to always see or hear who is coming and going and when.   She leaves her door ajar about two inches.

I used to think it was to let people feel they were

welcome to come in at will, but it is actually to enable her to hear everything and see everything without being seen.

Amusingly enough, over the last few weeks, I learned she is not nosy and has no problem minding her own business. Rather, the house and Wallie are her business, and she manages them well. She pays all the house expenses and is his first line of defense.

Strangely, I appreciate her position. It's an honest one that requires loyalty, and I have found she has that. Unlike Jason.

That one meeting. Everything feels different. He did it. Started the wheels turning again. I liked not thinking. Not figuring out or plotting. My brain rested and I want to live like that. Why couldn't he leave me with that?

I would have walked back in here and just relished in its beauty. Blake tries to take my jacket.

"No, thank you, Blake. If Wallie asks, I'll be in the tank." I say.

"The tank, Sir.?"

"The basement."

"Of course, Sir."

I pass Wallie's office and the same suited gentlemen are there again. Different suit, same sneaky look. He smiles this time. Maybe he figures I will be around a while so smiling may be to his benefit.

I turn discreetly to Blake, my back to the man, and speak.

"Blake, does he always wait in Wallie's office?"   I ask.

"Yes.   Once a week."   Blake looks at me as if he has something he wants to say.

Blake's holding his opinion. I see what he's thinking. It's not a good idea, but Blake is wise enough to not overstep his boundaries.

"Perhaps, he would be more comfortable in the parlor?"   I say.

Blake smiles. He doesn't trust him either. I will make the offer, Sir. Blake smiles, enters the office.

A new wind is blowing.   I'm just not sure if it's a good one or not. If I take the elevator, it will put me right into the room and bypass the security check, but I feel weird about waiting for an elevator with two perfectly good legs. I used them plenty in my old building where the elevator never worked.

I'm no stranger to steps.   My last residence made taking the steps a way of life. Descending the steps, I hear Mrs. Bird's footsteps walking toward Wallie's office.

I pause, my eyes level to floor behind a large floor vase. She glances toward the steps I am on, but doesn't see me, then walks into the office to the small-eyed man, excuses Blake and shuts the door.

I continue to the tank. I slept down here a few times. It's a great place.   The windows overlook the green grounds and the pool.   The entire glass wall can fold back, opening the lab to the massive deck behind the house.

For the first time, I walk to the window and just stand there. My hands are warm in my pockets and I know it drives Blake crazy when I wear my jacket in the house, but that's me. I'll take it off when I want to.

What if Jason is right? What if Wallie's father had something to do with my parent's death? What if Wallie knew about it all along? I wish all these questions weren't whirling around in my head now.

Jason said it himself. He is an agent first. He would do and say anything to get my cooperation, even shake my base. His motive is tainted. He wants his wife home and will pull all means to make that happen. He wants to close things up properly and find our mastermind. We have the same motive. We want to find the same person. Whoever and wherever they may be. Is he using me, or am I using him?

I like the new vision Wallie laid out. He is thinking about a legacy, something that never crossed my mind while trying to survive. I see no other motive for him. It's not money, that's for certain.

I walk to the planning board. What's this? Wallie has a Mexico marked on the rotating globe. What if this mission somehow connects him to the mastermind? No. That makes no sense. It wouldn't be wise to embark on something that may lead directly to you. I'm going with my gut. It hasn't failed me yet.

I unlock the phone Jason gave me to see the details of the case.

Coordinates. Jason's encrypted way of letting me know where it is. I think I saw a device in here somewhere. I look inside a cabinet. Here it is. I punch in the coordinates.

"Mexico," I say to myself.

The address of the President of Mexico's private residence. Reading through the details pulls me right back into the mindset I had in the Monastery when Jason first revealed the details of the Beaston Project.

That sinking, pulling feeling sets in. I want to go back into rest mode, but I can't help but feel curious about him now. He knows more than what's on this device for certain. He knew Jason would call. I can't help but feel that he is holding back pieces of the puzzle.

Questions are popping into my mind faster than the answers. I can't help but wonder if he knows about Jean too. I couldn't have gotten as far as I did in the last case if it wasn't for her.

It doesn't matter now if she was or wasn't my sister. She's dead. Yet, it bothers me thinking Jason is withholding from me. What else is he not saying?

Reading this mission detail is like looking at a half-sketched painting. There's so much missing. It's a series of bones. He gave me just enough to spark my interest and make me want to get involved, but not enough to satisfy my curiosity. Anyone can do a rescue mission. If I could, I would hand this phone back to him.

Mission Two:

"Convince the Mexican President to release the target (Christian Bleu) immediately.

Offer Exchange- Our cooperation in restoring peace in his region.

Order: DO NOT ENGAGE T. B."

When they bold a command, I have to wonder. T. B. is Tempest Bleu, Christian Bleu's wife. Jason knows that the longer she's there, her survival chance decreases drastically.   Why would they leave her? I want to be a party to a woman left to die.

"Hey," says Wallie walking into the Think-Tank loosening his tie. "Blake told me you were down here. You know, there's a whole house up there. You've slept down here all week."   Wallie says coming through the sliding door.

That door's movement is silent except for the swoosh of the air pump opening and closing it.

I slip the phone into my pocket. Wallie sits in the single recliner facing me.

He presses a discreet button.   The top of the small side table beside him ascends, revealing six different frosty drinks. A refrigerator embedded in the table, clever. He spins the display, selects one, and offers it to me.

I take it.   He opens one for himself and taps the top of the dispenser. It descends silently.

"Where d'you go?   I wanted you to come with me to the office."   He puts the bottle to his lips and takes a drink. He notices my countenance.   "I see you've had your meeting."

I cross my legs, putting my right ankle on my left knee and sink into the chair. Intentionally serious. I want answers.

"I don't play games. Tell me what you know. Until I know everything, I am not taking this mission. I'm no pawn." I say.

"Christian Bleu, 'the secret keeper'. In very particular circles, that is what he is known as. Christian designed this house." Wallie takes a drink. "Every security measure thought of with that brilliant thing between his two ears."

Now, I'm impressed. He has my attention.

"Why should I risk my life to rescue him? To preserve the secrets of some rich people who probably wouldn't bother to kick me if I were down? Not enough."

"And I concur. However, you are not preserving their secrets. You would preserve a man worth saving. Did you stop to wonder how a man gains the trust of these kinds of people? Not by gimmick. He just 'is' honesty, loyalty and trust rolled into one.

He will be being tortured for the location of his master-safe. He designed it and made it unobtainable by the average thief. They wouldn't know where to begin to look. He prepared to die to protect the secrets of his clients.

"So why not let some of these rich clients send their men to get him?"

"Trust. These people are corporate enemies. They don't play nicely in the sandbox. They're always trying to buy the sand. Also, leverage. Having Christian change provides obscene leverage.

There is a contract we sign. If a client is found to move against Christian, their deepest, darkest secrets will appear all over the news. You can't bribe the wealthy. Christian broke the narrative and got them to respect him.

His wife, Tempest Bleu, is still in Mexico. They won't bring her home. She's secondary in their eyes. She's on her own Caleb in the middle of a coup in Mexico with American's disappearing by the dozens.

I met her once. She's not a street-smart lady. She bakes apple pies for the Sunday school class she teaches."

"Apple pie huh." Recalling the smell of mom's fresh-baked pies on Sunday afternoon.

I never shared that with Wal. I take a drink and we both notice the sky darken through the large windows.

"His abduction is still unknown to his clients. If it comes out, there will be a ripple effect that will even hit the stock market."

"How did you find out?"

"I told you, I do my homework." A light flickers in his eyes as he leans forward, resting his elbows on his knees. "I want to do what others can't do so I have to know what others don't know."

He has a passion for this. I wonder what the secret keeper knows about the Davenports.

"With all the other abductions in Mexico, no one is

has narrowed down on Christian Bleu. He needs to be found and fast."

Funny, I'm thinking more about his wife as the one worthy to be rescued. She's the one that they will make a casualty of war. Purposely abandoned for their cause. Frankly, I couldn't give a rat's behind about keeping their secrets. I care about saving lives, though. I saw my mother afraid of the bumps in the night when dad was away. I saw her slide his shotgun under her bed as soon as he left. She shouldn't have had to do that. I need to think.

I take a sip of the drink and steady the bottle on my thigh with my hand on top of it. He couldn't have been captured by a client. Whoever took him had nothing for Christian to disclose.

Why leave his wife? She would have been great leverage to use against Christian? Tempest Bleu. She's the reason I will do this. I'll get him out too.

First, I have one person I need to talk to. Christian Bleu's partner. I want to look him in the eye. I'm meeting him in California, my next stop, Mexico. The flight was fast. I chose a hotel that would be impressive enough for this guy to consider seeing me. I have a feeling he will check.

"Lind McClean," I mutter.

I put on my leather jacket, zip my duffel bag and put it on the dresser. A habit, I look at the dresser mirror. No cracks. I will never forget the crack in the mirror.

You know a place is home when you miss it, when you leave and can't wait to get back. I miss the basement already.

This hotel is nice, expensive and elegant. The hot shower felt good. I had lunch in the dining room purposely so McLean's' spies could see me. I ate long enough for them to update him.   My cell phone rings.

"Yes," I say.

"Mr. Promise, your transportation is here."   Says the hotel desk clerk.

"I didn't request any."

I hang up, grab my bag and go to the lobby. A stretch limousine is waiting in front of the hotel, capped driver standing beside the back door.

"Mr. Promise?"   asks the driver.

The limousine is black, Mercedes, unmarked.

"Yes."

He opens the door.   It's Mr. McLean.   I get in.

"I hope this isn't too forward of me.   When my secretary told me we had a meeting, I assumed this was about Christian.   I thought it best we speak in private. I am worried sick about him, and his wife."

The car moves. I have never been to California.   The tall palm trees tower over us, lining the street.   He's a mature man.   Scruff, as if he hasn't shaved in days. He's wearing glasses. They aren't his everyday pair.   They look brand new and match his suit. He's a dresser. Nails manicured, newly manicured. So he's not that worried about his partner.

There is no glare on his glasses and I'm glad I can see his eyes. He takes out a cigarette and lights it. Diamonds surrounding his pendant style pinkie ring flash in the sunlight.

The limousine reeks of smoke. This must be his usual. It's in the leather too. His cell phone is on a charging pad and there is classical music playing in lightly in the background. A glass of whiskey half empty is in the cup holder beside him with three cigarette butts in a glass ashtray.

"Where is Christian?" he asks concerned.

"What makes you think he's missing?" I say.

"One thing Christian is responsible. I tried to contact him regarding a project we are in the middle of and he never got back to me."

"How long have you known him?" I ask.

He huffs and looks like he's digging into the archive of his mind.

"A long time. We graduated from MIT together. Massachusetts Institute of Technology. I struggled together after graduate school, sharing an apartment and cold Chinese food. Finally, Christian got a good job at a leading firm and paid the bills while I started our firm. When it got up and running, he left his job and joined me full time and we became partners. The rest is obvious. The most sought after Architectural and design company in the world."

"Because of Christian," I say. It's time to make him sing to my tune. I don't have time to play with him.

It pulls him out of his sentimental state and I see his guards go up. Guys like him don't sing back-up. They have to be right in front with the microphone in the spotlight.

"What did you say?"

"Because of Christian. If it weren't for him starting the business, you would be nowhere. Is that true?" I say, looking straight into his eyes.

"Yes. I guess you could say that. He was the driving force moving us forward. I'm grateful. He had guts to try new things."

"Had?" He's referring to Christian as if he is dead.

This guy reeks of guilt.

"Well, I mean, back then. Listen, is this an interrogation or do you want information that will help you find my friend? A man grows less spontaneous with time, with age, with a wife and family. You wouldn't know that, I imagine." He says glancing at my bare ring finger.

"Christian and I were risk-takers, college loans to pay

back yet we started a business, but after he married, and I married, the chance went out the window you see. We made sure steps."

"Did he tell you about his travel plans?"

"He did, in his way. He left a file on his desk of the projects he was working on. It has enough information to get through the next two weeks. So, two weeks was the length of his expected absence. If you're asking if I knew of his flight, or hotel, no. No one ever knew that. Christian had access to the private jet but knew it meant at least five people would know his where-about. He opted for a more discreet method. Public transport. When ever he went away, he would check in with me after two days. He hasn't. He's missing. So, my question to you is. Where is Christian Bleu?"

I can't help but feel there is another reason he didn't want to meet at his office. What didn't he want me to see?

"You said partner-ship. Fifty-fifty?"

"Yes. From the start."

"Who were Mr. Bleu's top three clients."

He chuckles.

"You know nothing about the way we operate, do you? Everyone knows that the unique aspect of our firm is secrecy and privacy.

Our clientele never come to our office and we rarely go to them. Transactions are done electronically, and any footprint of the interactions, discarded. We do not hold any footprint of the interactions in our firm. Thus, Christian doesn't know my clients, and I don't know his. It's a safe-keep for both of us. We only discuss mutual projects. They are rare and are upon request of the client."

"Why are they rare?"

"Cost. Only our elite customers willing to pay for the service of having both of us work on a project will request this.

Mr. Promise, if you're thinking one of our clients decided to 'off' Christian, you are off the track. None of them gain anything in his death or mine. They lose a great deal of information that they paid a great deal of money to get. You could say, it's another one of our safe-keeps."

"With so much on the line, in a fifty-fifty split, I imagine you had life insurance policies on one another," I ask.

"We do. Mutually."

He doesn't seem phased by that question at all. He walked through this line of questioning in his head already. If he had anything to do with Christian's disappearance, he undoubtedly thinks he has covered his tracks.

"I think we are wasting time here." He smashes his cigarette into the ashtray.

It is smashed differently from the others. The tip of the other cigarettes are facing the other side of his seat. Someone else was here, and recently. No lipstick, a man.

"What about Christian's wife?"

"Tempest is the love of his life. I have never seen two people more made for one another than they." he lights another cigarette, "I'm jealous. She was his college sweetheart.

His marriage lasted. My last two didn't. To heart, I want what I'm not truly made for. Christian is the settling type.

Dear God, what she must be going through." He shakes his head and looks out the window.

"How long were they married?"

"Oh, must be twenty-some-odd years. I've lost track. She's loyal." He looks directly at me. "If ever there was a woman loyal, it is her to the core. That's a dead-end for you, I'm afraid. Christian has everything left to her in his Will, and she knows it.

He would give her everything and anything dead or alive, but she's utterly dependent, you know, in personality. Timid. Afraid of her own shadow. She wouldn't dare cut him off. He's her lifeline."

"What do you mean dependent? Is she handicap?" I ask.

"Oh no. I mean, she's... emotionally dependent.

She has panic attacks and things like that. The opposite of her name, kind to a fault. He calls her 'my still waters'. And well, Christian has stuck up for her his fair share of times. People walk all over her. She attracts disrespect like a magnet.

I hate to end this abruptly, but I have a meeting in ten minutes." He looks at his Rolex watch.

"What do you want to say that you haven't said already?" I ask, feeling the limousine come to a stop.

He leans in toward me. He looks down at the intercom button and makes certain it is off and the driver can't hear us.

"A few days before Christian left, he told me he was taking on a new project. It was rare for him, this late in the year, to do this. He said it couldn't be helped, and that this was a huge deal. He wanted me to take up one of his other projects he almost finished so he could meet this new deadline. He said at this stage, it wouldn't matter. This broke our safe-keep.

For Christian to do this, it had to be a tremendous deal with lots of implications. In all the years of our partnership, he never broke a safe-keep."

"Do you have any idea who that new client is? Think, did you walk in on a phone call... see an appointment book?"

"No, he told me, nothing more. I felt you should know. I thought, perhaps, when he didn't return, that he was meeting this person. I don't know, it's far-fetched but my mind has been spinning since he left." He rubs his forehead.

"Where does his disappearance leave you? Business-wise." I ask.

"In a bind, to say the least. I couldn't possibly hire anyone to complete his projects. They are all encrypted and stored off-sight known only to Christian.
If Christian doesn't return, it is the end of the business. The wealthy don't give second chances. I need Christian or at the least, his access. So, you see, I have no reason to him harm. No motive, as you say."

"I am not a cop, Mr. McLean."

"If you were, I would not be speaking to you."

He presses a button, and the driver walks around and opens the door. He gets out of the vehicle, then turns to the driver.

"Take Mr. Promise where ever he wants to go." He tells the driver. "My meeting awaits. I hope I was of service to you, Caleb Promise. Contact me the moment you know anything."

"I will," I say.

He enters the front of a glass skyscraper building at least twenty stories high with an ambiguous company emblem on it.
The driver gets back into the limousine, which I'm sure

is bugged and asks me where to.

"The airport." I say.

California is an interesting place, but I have a feeling that what's waiting for me in Mexico is far more interesting.

The news is showing closure of all transports between the U.S. and Mexico. That's the benefit of having a billionaire with unhinged access and access to private flights.

My flight will be private but masked to look like a charity bringing in medical supplies. Not entirely fake. Wal had his jet loaded with food goods and a staff in matching t-shirts. They think I'm a journalist along to capture the optics. I guess my clothes fit that bill. Brown leather jacket, blue jeans, gray form-fitting shirt.

The television on-board shows chaos in the streets of Mexico. I grind my boot heels into the carpet of the plane. I have a feeling this will be a turbulent ride.

CHAPTER SEVEN

Tempest Bleu
Present Day

Lord, please… that's all that I can think of saying. My heart is pounding louder than the fake officers banging on the door.

I lean my weight against the door, bracing it, as it is the weaker of the two. The fake officer rams against it while turning the knob. I jump.

I put my hand over my mouth. The door-nob on the connecting door jiggles. One kick and he could easily breach the door.

"Policia. Open now!" pounding.

Jeff eases to the desk and quietly unscrews the shade off a lamp, pulls its chord out and holds it from the top. Bouncing its heavy base, he squeezes it tightly, balancing the weight. He bites his bottom lip, and his face turns red from anger. I know he would unleash revenge on them for what they did to his wife. They stop banging, but the shadow of their feet is beneath the doors.

Suddenly, the screw from the lamp rolls off of the desk. It falls. It hits the carpet with a thud.

Jeff and I look at each other. Did they hear it? Beneath the door, the shadow of their feet. The shadows are still. No. Thank God the television was up so loud.

I shut my eyes and pray. That's all I can do. We freeze. We wait, barely breathing.

The doorknob releases, returning to its normal position. Footsteps are going down the hall and the sound of something dragging. Jeff lowers his lamp and looks through the peep-hole. I take my turn afterward.

They are each pulling the rude woman. Each holding a forearm. Her feet flopping side to side as they jerk her body. Her head tosses, bobbing as they go.

"They're gone," I say to Jeff.

He puts down the lamp, runs his fingers through his hair, then goes into the bathroom and washes his face. My breath is short and my heart won't stop racing. The room spins. I brace my hand on the door, shut my eyes. Jeff is upholding me from the side.

"Come on, it's okay." He whispers.

He leads me to the sofa. I shut my eyes and lean my head back to get some air. My hair soaked with perspiration sticking to my face and my blouse is wet beneath the arms, but my hands are ice cold. Jeff places a wet washcloth on my head. He's a good one. My mind is resting. I'm exhausted.

I open my eyes but can't see. There's something on my eyes. How long have I been asleep? I reach up and take it off. It is a washcloth. Where am I? I'm not home. Now I remember. I was hoping it was all a bad dream. A memory. But it's not. I'm awake and this is the reality.

I'm still on the sofa in Jeff's hotel room. I shut my eyes, hoping to leap back to that moment when Christian and I were at home. I would change our plans and go to Singapore as he suggested. But I can't. I'm stuck in reality. A dark, horrid reality.

Helpless. That's what I am. That's what I imagine Jeff feels. He has said little and I don't know what to say to him anymore. He's living what I fear. I fear finding Christian's body in the middle of the street, tortured and alone. What can I say to Jeff? Perhaps it's better if I leave him to his thoughts. He left the television on loudly just in case the fake cops came back. I wish we could turn it off. It's making me crazy listening to it and seeing constant images of the rioting in the streets.

"Look, Tempest," Jeff says.

I sit up. He's leaning forward in his seat across from me. His satellite phone still in hand.

He changed his shirt. Thank God. I couldn't stomach that blood splatter. The newscaster is speaking Spanish, but the subtitles are in English.

"The United States is holding its position. The evacuation of American's from Mexico has been successful so far but it is believed there are many still in Mexico but are not reachable because of the rioting that has broken out in the streets.

The Mexican Police are overwhelmed by vandalism, rioting and individual calls for help from those caught in this very unstable time. The Mexican President made a statement just moments ago. I quote, "Rebels are to blame for the rash actions leading to this unrest in our beautiful country. We are negotiating with the United States to ensure American lives are not lost. For now, we advise Americans still in Mexico to stay where they are. As a precaution, the United States Embassy is closed and all travel between Mexico and the United States has ceased until further notice."

Jeff and I look at each other. He picks up the phone and calls the front desk. Still no dial tone.

"Anything?" I whisper.

"No. Nothing." He says low. "I wonder if they are all gone. The bad guys, I mean."

"Jeff, what should we do? They took her, just took her. People just don't do that."

I put my feet on the floor and tuck my hair behind my ears, straighten my blouse and peek at the cut on the back of my hand.

"How did you get that?" Jeff asks.

I think he's trying to take his mind off the circumstances at hand. I just realized I have blood drops on the right thigh of my pants. The cut on the back of my hand brings it all comes back to me. Shoved through the crowd outside of the American Embassy, my hand grazed the wooden stick of a woman's protest sign saying "PEACE OR BLOOD". Ironic, really. There is no peace, and I got the blood.

"Nothing. I'm fine."

He stands and walks past me. I'm grateful for Jeff. My Lord, if I were alone, I don't know what I would do. The tears are rolling again. I am scared. So afraid I can barely think or move. I wish my dearest Christian were here. He would know what to do.

If all the world came against us in this hotel, I would still feel safe if he were here. He has a knack for staying calm in a crisis. I think it is his relationship with God. I have one too, but I am so alone. I don't think I ever realized how much I depend on him until this happened.

I want to run out of these doors and through the street banging on every door looking for my love, but how can I? I'm afraid of every shadow. Would it help?

What makes me think I can do more than the police? I wish we never came here now. It was my idea. The guilt is overwhelming. If we never came to Mexico, Christian would be here now. If I listened to him and went to Singapore, none of this would be happening.

Gunshots rivet outside. We don't want to move the curtains for fear of someone seeing the curtains move. It is late. It must be dark outside. I cover my ears and weep. I must hold it together. I can't afford for Jeff to tire of me. He's the only one helping me. I take my hands off of my ears to wipe my nose and it is silent. The room is black. What has happened? I still hear gunshots outside, but the television has stopped, and the lights went off.

"Jeff?"   I whisper.

I wipe my face and try to blink my eyes.

The clock in the room is off. The television is off, and the room is in total darkness.

"Jeff?   Answer me, please."

No answer. I stand quietly. I can't make a sound. Dear Lord, my heart starting to pound louder. I slip my flats on and adjust my top that has bunched up under my arms. Not a sound in the other room still. Did he leave me? Did Jeff slip out?

No, he wouldn't! What if he did.   He owed me nothing. After all, he lost his wife and may not be thinking of anything but his survival.   He has a better chance without me. I was just dead weight to him, anyway. Oh, Lord, I'm alone.

"Jeff?   Please, if your..."   I whisper ambling, my trembling hands extended, groping aimlessly through the darkness.

Curtains, I'm at the window. I have to open the curtains. I have to take the chance. The room is dark.   Slowly, I pull the rod and the curtains open, the glow from the moonlight reveals the room. There is a figure standing in the bathroom doorway.

I open my mouth to scream when it steps into the light. It's Jeff.   He puts his finger to his lips to shh me. He has gauze in his hand. He takes my hand and wraps my cut.

"I thought you left me." I exhale.

Jeff puts his hands on my shoulders and looks at me directly.

"Tempest, I will not leave you. We're getting out of here together."

"What do we do? We can't call downstairs, we can't leave-"

"We have to try. With the power out, the locks don't work. Anyone can walk in here. If anyone's downstairs, that's our hope."

"What about your father's men? They may come up here looking for you and if you're not here-" I say, trying to find a reason to stay in this familiar setting.

What's out there is far more terrifying than being in here.

"-It's been hours. They're not coming." He looks disappointed but determined.

I need his strength now, but I don't think I can set foot out of this room.

"Here's the plan," Jeff steps backward gesturing with his hands as he speaks, "we go downstairs and check it out. If no one's there, we go to the police station.
It's about a mile away. I passed it earlier, it's better than

sitting here. No electricity, no locks, we're waiting to be slaughtered. Besides, the battery on the satellite phone died a half-hour ago." He says holding it up to me.

"Why didn't you tell me?"

"I didn't want to worry you. This is our chance." He says sticking the phone in his trouser pocket.

"Wait, Jeff, all buildings like this have a back-up generator. It's supposed to kick in when the power goes out... unless..."

"Unless what?" he asks interested.

"Unless someone disabled it. But there is a manual re-start. Every generator has one."

"How do you know all this?"

"My Christian. Trust me. The generator is in the basement or on the roof. If we get power, we get locked doors and we get your phone charged to call for help.
Jeff, also, we may not be alone. Hotels usually have a panic room for the head staff. The staff is probably in it right now."

Jeff is thinking. Despite all I know, I don't think I would have the guts to do this if Jeff were not with me.

"All right. Let's go. Let's do it. First, we find the panic room. Then, the generator." He puts on his sneakers. "Do you have any quiet shoes? Something you can run in?"   he asks, looking at my feet.

"No. I don't."   I say.

"Wait, my wife may."   Jeff goes into her luggage.
"Here.   Try these on."

I don't have the heart to tell him, but just looking at
them, I can tell they are not wide width.   I try to push my
foot into it so he knows that they don't fit.

A noise.   What was that?   We glance at each other.
Silently, I slip my foot back into my shoes.   The noise is
getting closer.   It sounds like someone rustles through
things.
Doors and drawers opening and slamming.   Whoever
that is, they may be the same ones that cut the power.

"We need to go. Now."   Says Jeff wide-eyed.

I'm terrified.   What if they catch us in the hall like the
rude   woman?   He   pushes   me   gently   toward   the
adjourning door we open it.

"Come-on, come-on."   Says Jeff standing in the
doorway looking in the noise's direction to our right.

"Oh, passports."   I pull the door open.   The safe
lock released when the power went out.   I grab my
passport and Christians and stick them into my bag then
run in the bathroom, snatch Christian's medication and
shove it in my bag too.
Jeff pulls his head in from the hall quickly and leans into
my ear.

"They're in my room."   He says.

"Stay close to the wall.   Now."

I'm in front of him. He moves me along with his hand on my shoulder. I feel his palm guiding my direction like a man leading a woman in a dance.

Left, right, a slight pull on my shoulder means stop. It helped me. It helped me step into that hall where a woman was dragged away.

We move quickly. A few steps to the next door well. Stop. A few more steps. Tuck into the next door-well, stop. A well-timed dance.

We make it about three rooms down.   The elevator is four doors away around the corner.   Jeff pauses.   Listens. They stopped rummaging. Our eyes meet and we know they may come our way.

"In here."   He whispers, pointing me to the room my back is pressed against.

I turn the handle, and it opens. Thank God the power is out. The darkness covers us. I need a lot of covering.

We step inside.   The room is empty.   No one has been in there yet.   Their luggage is in-tact and drawers, closed. Silly, but I am angry.   I don't want anyone touching Christian's things.

We press ourselves against the wall.   Jeff peaks through the peep-hole and I listen.   Then fumbling and zippers opening.   I   visualized   them   rummaging   through Christian's luggage. Anger rises in me to think of them touching his things. A useless anger that goes nowhere.

We listen, they are in another room. The bustling noise starts again.

"Now." Says Jeff opening the door and pulling me by the arm into the hallway.

Jeff is focused. He says nothing and we get two more doors down and then silence falls again.

"This is taking too much time! You take the next one, I'll go across the hall." Says one thief to the other in a thick accent.

The man walks in our direction. If it were not dark, he would see us. There is a beam of light from his flashlight waving behind us. It's getting closer.

Jeff pauses and urges me to the room across the hall. I turn the handle and push. The door resists. The lock is open, but something is jamming it from opening. Jeff pushes, nothing. The door is bouncing back our way.

He is in the hall. Just two doors away. We can't run. They will catch us. They won't stop looking until they find us. He has a flashlight in one hand and a gun slung around his shoulders. We push again. Nothing. He's coming.

"Check it out!" the thief in the room says to the man. He stops and goes back toward the man in the room.

Jeff and I push hard and the door gives-way. It opens. My Lord! A stench, so suffocating and thick causes both of us to gag.

Two bodies. An elderly couple. The man's eyes still open. They were shot. Probably days ago. I think I may vomit. My God, I have never seen a dead body.

"Que es Esto!" a thief asks. (What was that?).

"I'll check it out." Says the thief with a gun.

Jeff pushes me into the bathroom and signals me to close the door. He leaves the door slightly open and pushes the bodies toward the door, preventing the door from opening further. Grabs the lamp and steps into the closet.
The thief pushes the door with the nuzzle of his gun. It bounces back, blocked by the bodies. The stench stops him.

"Caramba! Stinks!" he backs out of the room. "Todo muerto. They are all dead."

We wait. Silently wait. I cover my mouth and nose with my blouse, trying to smell through my perfume. Silence. The bathroom door opens.
It's Jeff. We tiptoe, step across the bodies back toward the door. We peek down the hall and their flashlights are going down the hall in the opposite direction.

"Nada." The thief reports.

We run out of the room and make a little further when we hear them stop fumbling again. We open another door. I am praying there are no dead bodies in here. I hate this. I'm sweating profusely. A couple armed with lamps and the hotel iron stop when they realize we are American.

My heart is thumping. I am so glad to see people. Alive people. A couple. They are young. Younger than Jeff and obviously younger than me. But they are here. We aren't alone. If they are here, there must be others.

"Shh," I say holding my hands up to them while Jeff peeks through the hole. Christians handkerchief is sticking out of my cleavage area where I stuck it. I tuck it in and turn to them.

"Come with us, we're going downstairs," I say.

"Are you crazy?" asks the young lady.

Why do people keep asking me that?

"They are right there. We are stronger together. Come with us." I say.

"Tempest, we have to move." Says Jeff turning from the peep-hole. "If they don't want to come. We leave them." Says Jeff. His eyes glancing at them, knowing their fate.

He's right and I know it, but I hate to see them stay here. I look at the stubborn young lady. She crosses her arms and shakes her head. I nod at Jeff. We know what will happen. I step up behind Jeff and put my hand on his shoulder.

"Now." He whispers.

We open the door and move. We pass two doors.   Then turn the corner.   There they are. The elevators. What am I doing?   Out of habit, I push the down button.

"Here."   Says Jeff waving his arm frantically for me to come to the stairwell.

No sooner do we step inside of the stairwell and close the door controlling the doorknob from clicking, there is pounding on a door. A scream. Not me. The young lady.

Jeff touches my hand to ease me. There is a small window in the stairwell door. He rises and looks through it. Light illuminates his face. His light eyes serious and red. He looks down at me crouched on the floor.

"We can't help them now." He says.

"I know," I say.

Gunshots. The young lady screams 'NO' in the most shrilling way. They must have killed the man. She is valuable. She's screaming his name. Then she screams for help… no… don't. She's screaming, 'you hear me! Help me!'. Will they realize? Will she tell them about us trying to negotiate her freedom that will never come?

Jeff and I glance at each other and start descending the steps quickly and quietly.   We realize that the stairwell is the only way up and down so we will likely share it with thieves, kidnappers and whoever else is taking advantage of the power outage.

My heart is pounding.   Jostling down these steps isn't helping.   My breathing is getting short.   I keep thinking

I'm hearing footsteps behind us.

We make it down at least five flights. Why did we want a room with a view? We figured that this time, since we couldn't afford it for our real honeymoon, that we would get the best room with the best view as high up as possible.

Finally. We're in the lobby. The door opening to the lobby is half glass. We stare through the door. The lobby is dark. Vague light makes its way through the lobbies large broken glass windows.

It looks nothing like it did when Christian and I checked in. It was shiny, clean and buzzing with travelers arriving. The large stone flowerpots beside the towering square pillars overflowing with fresh arrangements and a floral scent filled the air.

Now, it looks like a bomb hit it. Most of the lobby furnishings broken or on fire. It looks like a nightmare. Is that blood splatter? It is? How can this be?

Abandoned suitcases and purses litter the floor as if a frantic exodus took place. An exodus I wish we were a part of now. If I left, I would feel total guilt and would be sick watching this from my safe bedroom in the States, wondering if Christian is in it.

Outside, are those... yes! Police cars. Their lights blink brightly in the darkness. They are right there. What if those are the officers Mr. Douglas sent?

The lobby seems empty. All we have to do is get to the police cars, they will take us to the station and I can call for help. Oh, our nightmare is over. I'm sure Mr. McLean can get me home.

"I don't see anyone," I whisper to Jeff.

"Me either. There are police lights." He says eyes locked on the police cars.

Jeff is not smiling, why? No sooner does he say it, three armed men walk right past the stairwell door. Jeff flattens himself against the wall out of the window view, and I shut my eyes. We can hear their talking fade as they turn the corner.

I want the police to see them. Arrest them. They are heading in that direction. Emotion floods over me. We are so close to freedom.

I put my hand over my mouth and weep. Right about now, my husband would have placed his open palm on my back and pressed gently, letting me feel the heat from his hand. I have to pull it together. If I jeopardize our escape, I will never forgive myself. Probably because I'll be dead.

I exhale and wipe my eyes before Jeff can even notice. I stand. We watch, nothing. We don't see them. We don't see anyone in the lobby.

Carefully, Jeff opens the door and we go toward the police lights. Just about thirty feet from the exit. I see the police lights growing stronger. We get to the center of the lobby and we both stop.

Our arms drop limp at our sides and all our hopes dreams are dashed. The police cars are on fire and the lights are still spinning. Two bodies sit slumped in the front seats, burning.

Slowly, we ease toward the exit to leave the hotel when

a vehicle pulls up to the hotel entrance. Their guns sticking out of the windows. My hopeful smile drops, and Jeff points to the office door behind the counter.

"There, the office. Go." Jeff says.

We have no choice. We approach the office door, Jeff puts his hand on the doorknob. I'm close to his back, but a buzzing sound of flies distracts me. I turn, peer at the floor behind the front desk counter. Why did I look?

The bodies of the three clerks that were doing their shift. Bloody shot in the face, flies swarming around them. The warm night air mixed with hot decaying blood. Suddenly, the front desk telephone rings.

Someone is coming to the office door from inside the office. Jeff lifts his hand off the knob. We turn, run to the other side of the desk and squat on the floor in front of the front desk. A gunman comes out of the office, steps over the bodies as if they weren't even there and leans over the counter, looks at the ringing phone at the room number.

"Guillermo. We got another one! Room 565. I told you. We fix the phone line then, stay here, they call us!" he laughs.

Guillermo comes out of the office chewing, holding a machine gun, nozzle up. The first gunman hits Guillermo in the chest playfully.

"The last girl got us three thousand dollars. Don't wound this one. I want top dollar. Got it?" The gunman says to Guillermo.

They cock their guns. They have to walk right past us to

go to the stairwell. If they look backward for any reason, the phone ringing, a sound, anything, we are dead.

They step out from behind the front desk and head toward the stairwell. I pray. 'Dear Lord, don't let them see us.' Just then, from bending, Jeff's satellite phone falls from his pocket. I reach to catch it; it bounces off my palm. It falls.

It hits the floor. But God is on our side. Just then, a group of rioters appear walking walk past the front of the hotel yelling and shooting their guns into the air. Their noise masks the bang of the phone that falls from Jeffs pocket. Jeff scoops it up. The armed men playfully return fire, shooting in the air inside the hotel. We keep our backs to the counter and quickly dodge the bodies and go into the office and close the door quietly behind us.

We exhale. Dear Lord, if the phone didn't ring, we would have walked right into that back-office room. I shut my eyes and take a breath. When I open them, Jeff is already walking around in the office. I rush in after him and close the door behind me.

There are two desks, computers on them, and the back wall has monitors for the security cameras in the hotel. They are dark gratefully. If they were on, they would have seen us coming. Jeff is moving so quickly he almost looks panicked. He's making me nervous.

"Where is it! I don't see it. There's no panic room in here, Tempest." Jeff says, sweating.

"Let me look." I walk past him, hands shaking.

He's looking uneasy. He is so calm, but we are in a tight spot. He clasps both hands on top of his head, pacing the floor. He's looking through the one-way mirror on the wall. At least we can see if anyone is coming toward the office. But if they do, we have nowhere to go. We are unarmed. Jeff pulls out draws.

"What are you doing?" I ask Jeff from inside a coat closet.

"Looking for a weapon! You think those bastards wouldn't shoot us on sight." Jeff says harshly.

"Thank God, I don't have to worry about them dragging me up the hall," I say sticking my head out of the closet.

He stops and looks at me sarcastically. I shrug. Then my eyes move. Through the two-way mirror, the gunmen are in the lobby dragging a young woman through the lobby by her hair. She's kicking and screaming and scratching at his fist clamped around her blond hair.

Jeff looks as if he's wrestling within himself. She looks like his wife. I can see his impulse is to help her. She is fighting as hard as she can. Screaming help.

It would be inhumane to ignore another person's cry for help. I never imagined myself the type to put my safety before someone else's. But here I am, thinking there is no way we can go out there.

Jeff is getting lost in this. No doubt he's thinking about his wife. Is guilt is driving him toward this girl? He's inching toward the door.

In my heart, I know we should try, but in my head, I know it won't help. We would only be taken too. Jeff, would probably be killed. I can envision him lying on the ground out there with a bullet through his head and me trying to explain to his father why Jeff never made it out. He's moving closer toward the door.

"Jeff. You can't." I whisper.

He stops walking, but his eyes are locked on the scene. The girl breaks loose and runs. She accidentally runs into another gunman standing outside. He grabs her and slaps her with the back of his hand. She falls to the floor and doesn't get up. She's not moving. The larger gunman slings his rifle across his back by the strap, lifts her and throws her over his left shoulder like a sack of rice, smacks her on the bottom and walks out the front of the hotel.

The other guard lights a cigarette and leans on the front desk counter. As soon as they dispose of her, they will come back in here. Where is it? I go back into the closet. Christian said every panic room has a panel. A secret panel near the entrance in a simple construct. I am pressing parts of the closet's back wall, searching for it. Here it is!

Clever, a pressure plate that looks like a vent. I press it and the rear wall of the closet pops open. I hear voices getting close. They are right outside the door. No! Is it too late? The gunmen are approaching the desk.

"Jeff!" I whisper harshly.

He's in a daze. The panic room door is open. I have one leg inside the shallow closet. I have to get him. The gunman's hand is on the door.

I rush to Jeff, pull his shirt. He comes. We rush into the panic-room and Jeff quietly closes the closet door as we hear the office door open. Then a bang.

"Ah!" one gunman grunts.

"Que? What did you do, stupido?" asks the other.

"You left this draw open, idiot. This is my bad knee too!"

"No, I didn't."

The panic room is dark. Jeff is about to pull the panic room door shut. I put my hand on his gently, our signal to wait. We can't see each other. When the door shuts, the pressure plate in the closet will click. That's the spring mechanism reengaging the lock and resetting the pressure plate. If they hear it, it will only be a matter of time before they find this door.

I'm waiting. Something will happen. They will do something. When they do, I can mask the sound of the click. Not yet, not yet. I hear one moving. He's near the closet. My hands are trembling. He's in the closet. What is he looking for?

"It's in here, I saw it. Whiskey. You took it, didn't you?"

"So what?" he replies.

"Idiot!" he says angrily.

He slams the closet door. Now. I tap Jeff's hand. He pulls the door, and it reset.

"What the hell!"   says one gunman.

Oh, Lord, did he hear.?   What did he hear?

"Que?"   the other gunman asks.

"Look at this."   He says.

I hear the closet door open again and rustling in the closet.   Jeff and I back away from the door.   Jeff's fists are tight, and his jaw is sealed.

"Golf clubs.   These cost more than my car."

"What are you going to do with golf clubs, stupido?"   Laughs the other gunmen.

It is windowless, dark and silent. A panic room, if done well, is soundproof.   I can't see my hand in front of my face. A thought. Are we alone in here? If we are not, they would accept us?

I pull my husbands' handkerchief out of my cleavage and almost wipe my face with it, then stop myself.   I don't want it to lose its scent and I will never wash it.   I wipe the sweat from my head with the back of my sleeve. Slowly, I slide my hand along the wall near the door to find the light switch. I can't exhale. Not in the dark.

CHAPTER EIGHT

Caleb Promise
Present Day

The flight was bumpy. What could I expect flying with boxes of medication in a mini cargo plane? It sure isn't like flying private. Have I gone soft? Never. I grab my duffel bag, sling it over my shoulder, feeling the strap grip my brown leather jacket, I step onto the airstrip.

The sky is black tonight. Stars are clear just hanging in the sky. Flying at night, the lights of the city flickering. It's nice. Outside of the private airstrip gate, a line of taxis with their drivers stand cross-legged outside of their vehicles waving new arrivals toward their open taxi door.

I choose someone who looks like he is not a talker. I don't chatter. The ride is bumpy but quiet and faster than I expect. We pass clusters of people. Some involved in the protests, some going about their usual business.

The President's private residence is on security lockdown, but thanks to Jason's directions, I can get in. That's what made me listen to him when we met. I read the United States Embassy agents report while on the flight. Details of Christian's location just before he disappeared.

The taxi stops at the President's residence. Protesters are stacked at his gate waving signs and fists into the air. The President of Mexico's official guards are holding their position, securing the perimeter. I pull my cell phone out and call the number the President of Mexico handed me in Switzerland when we had our 'encounter' at the last mission.

It's warm, and the vibe is chaotic yet passionate. The driver is squeezing his steering wheel tightly. His knuckles turn white.

"Senor, we should not stay here." Says the taxi driver.

"One moment, Senor," I say listening to the phone ringing.

I've never been in a protest. I've been in a New York deli with an irate customer trying to climb over a counter and fight for a pickle. This is something entirely different. The feeling of intense determination is tangible. It would only take one person to flare and this scene will ignite into a fight.

It's loud. Lots of chanting. "Down with Ruiz!" Others bellow, "Long live Ruiz!" Banners supporting the President wave beside banners opposing him. A eight foot wrought-iron gate surrounds the property. Armed guards stand inside and outside of the gate, legs spread, gripping machine guns. It feels as if a cloud is hanging over the building.

I hang up. The United States media focused more on the disappearances of Americans in the region than this.

This problem is bigger than it appears in the U. S. media. It usually always is. I look at my watch. It's time. I tap the driver; he drives a few blocks and makes a few turns, stopping beside a grassy, overgrown field with abandoned cars and vacant buildings.

He's an older man. I'm surprised he's out here on a night like tonight. He looks around through the car windows then looks at me while taking the money I hand him.

"Seguro, Senor?" he asks me.

"Yes, I'm sure this is it. Thank you, Senor." I step out of the vehicle.

It's dotted with young men wearing bandannas tied around their necks. The street lights are broken out and an abandoned apartment building is with no windows.

"You get dead, Gringo." He says shaking his head as he drives away.

Firebombing forced President Ruiz from the Capital building into this supposedly secure residence. It is above a maze tunnels and hidden escape routes. He's isolated for his safety unless his greatest enemy is locked in with him.

I received a text with the location to go to. This does not differ from walking in an isolated area of Brooklyn at night. At least that's how it feels. I sling my duffel bag across my chest and the bag rests on my back. I walk street amid the darkness toward an abandoned building in the center of the field.

That didn't take long. Halfway to the building, I hear someone approaching. To my left, a motorbike is parked in front of the tall grass. It's shiny, clean and cared for. It hasn't been out here long. Neither has its rider coming up behind me dragging what sounds like a chain. This isn't where I want him, so I keep walking until we pass the tall thick grass and enter a clearing.

"Gringo! I can smell a new Gringo!" He yells.

He whistles. More footsteps. They step out of the tall grass. I keep walking. Almost there. It sounds like at least three more people. It was inevitable. The mouth never travels without the body. He will do all the talking. They will do what he says.

A gunshot. A can skips off the ground near my feet. I take three more steps to be right where I need to be. I stop and zip my jacket. I want to keep my shirt clean.

I and turn around slowly, hands lifted. Four guys. Twenty-something. Two easy drops. One visible gun. One knife. One chain. The mouth with the gun approaches first.

"What-ch-a got in that bag, Jeffe?'" he asks.

"Nothing for you." I answer flatly.

He does exactly what I wanted him to. He steps forward; I extend my foot, hook the back of his heel mid-stride and draw it back to me. His legs extend into a near split. Bringing his face right into my right elbow. I break his nose. My hand already on his gun and my finger behind the trigger. He drops. I dismantle the gun in one move.

"Ah! My nose!" He yells, rolling, dropping to his knees.

A swift kick from my boot to his chin. His head flails back, and I knock out him.

"You're dead." Yells a guy pulling his knife.

He lunges at me. Sweet momentum. I grab his arm and pull. His body leans forward. I grabbed his hand, wrench it backward. It opens, the knife drops. On his knees. One chop to the carotid artery. His body paused, goes limp, and he drops on his face in the grass. The other looks at his chain, drops it and runs. The other easy-drop runs with him.

I kick the gun parts into the tall grass, pat the guy with the broken nose's pockets and find them. The keys to the motorbike. I shove them into my jean pocket and unzip my jacket. The musty night's heat thickens the air.

I glance at my watch while walking toward the abandoned building. I don't have long. A stray dog barking in the distance, an occasional hot breeze, betray my knowledge of what's brewing in the heart of this city. If it were not for the distant chants and fire trucks dowsing small shops set ablaze, it would feel like a vacation. I push my hands in my pockets.

The hollow broken brick frame of the abandoned building festers with crawling things and moving shadows. The hot reek of urine rushes up my nostrils, but there is something else in here. Something rotten. There it is. Twisted in front of an old rusted file cabinet, uncovered eliminating curiosity.

A decaying body. Unidentifiable. Muddy. Someone that somebody may be searching for set here as a deterrent. My phone program says it's right there. It's behind the file cabinet. I step over the body and dark body fluids.

The locater dot turns green. I put my thumbprint on the lit box, and   something unlocks. I punch in the code on my locater and a full-body scanner light runs from my head to my feet.

Then, behind me, a soft click then repeated beeps speeding up. I walk toward the sound and step on a spot. A slab of concrete slides back open, revealing a ladder.

Habit, I look left, then right. I descend the ladder. When my foot touches the bottom rung; the slab slides shut over my head.

About a half of a mile walk through the dimly lit corridors, passing a few of the President's sweaty guards in the tunnel, I arrive, sweaty and dusty myself.

I reach the elevator flanked by two guards with heavy hands. One searches me with a locked eye and grit jaw, I bare their prodding.   I don't like being touched.

"I hope you enjoyed it. You won't do it again." I snatch my bag off the steel table away from the other guards prying hands.

The elevator door is steel. The guard puts in his key, turns it and it opens. The doors open. An armed guard is standing in the elevator.   I don't like elevators. Even in a President's safe house.   I think I got used to stairs from the elevator always being broken in my old residence.

As it ascends, I can hear faint chanting outside. I'm led from a private elevator into a large sitting room more representative of being a President's quarters.

Ornate paneling and fresco's on the wall. Fine vases with wilted flowers still in them. A guard takes my bag and frisks me again. It is as if things froze when the rioting began weeks ago.

The air-conditioning is on, but the pungent smell of the old flowers overwhelms the room. The walls are neutral, but bursts of color in paintings jump out at me. Faces of past Presidents who used this residence.

The lights are dim, purposely I believe. They don't cast shadows of anyone passing in front of them. Beside a window, President Ruiz's is Personal Adviser, Renaldo Gutierrez. His photo was in the brief Jason sent me.

He has been the United States' sole contact with Mexico. Apparently President Ruiz has refused direct contact with the President of the United States. He doesn't look pleased to see me at all. He looks me up, and down, then forces a fake smile, stepping toward me.

He has a notable scar going from his front hairline, crossing his eye and ending on the center of his cheek. He risked his life to save President Ruiz during an attack on the campaign trail. It made him popular with the people. The scar tells everyone how committed he is to his position and the people of Mexico.

I run my hand through my hair and adjust the front of my open leather jacket. I extend my hand. I don't represent myself on this trip; I represent the United States. Otherwise, my hand would stay in my pocket. On first glance, I don't like this guy. I know slippery when I see it.

"Hello, Mr. Gutierrez. Caleb- "I say to Gutierrez.

"What are you doing here?" his hands clasped behind his back. "The President is very busy... Mr. Promise."

Nice. It will be a long trip. I lower my hand.

"I can imagine. With all that going on out there, nowhere to go." I say sarcastically.

"You didn't answer my question." Says Gutierrez.

"Aware of that," I say looking around the room.

He doesn't like me, and I don't mean for him to. He was glancing at the danger outside but seems more trouble is in here. Fear is subjective, but lack of it is reasonable if you have no reason to fear. So why wouldn't the Personal Adviser to the most man hated, not fear reprisals if his boss were, dethroned? I don't like that answer spinning in my head. I'm not sure... yet.

The tall wooden door open and the President enters. The door is closed behind him and my eye catches a very curious worker studying my face as fast as he can before he shuts the door.

"Mr. Promise." Says President Ruiz. "I remember you well. Your eyes as blue as our waters." His hand extends. "A pleasure." I shake his hand accordingly. "I wish it were under better conditions, Mr. President."

"To what do I owe the pleasure of this visit. For now, I am avoided like a plague."

"I thought you may want a friendly visit."

The President puts his hand on my shoulder, leading me to the sitting area with two high-back chairs facing one another in front of an oversized fireplace.

"Do you need a place to stay?" looking at my duffel bag slung across my back. "Consider it done. You're in the safest place in Mexico."

I can feel Gutierrez's eyes on our backs.

"Please, have a seat." the President extends his hand. "You met Mr. Gutierrez?"

"Yes." I turn and glance at Gutierrez.

"Would you care for a drink?" asks the President.

"No, thank you."

My eyes wrap around the crystal liquor bottles on his bar. I wish I could forget, but I can't. The comfort of a cold, smooth glass in my hand. I can slide my fingers down the curves of the bottle at will. It gives when I want it to and goes with me willingly. The taste, the burn of that liquid sliding down my throat unobstructed. I look away. It cannot become real to me again. Breaking free from its grip, difficult the first time. I can't imagine the difficulty level trying to break it a second time.

"Mr. Gutierrez, would you check on those things we discussed earlier?" asks the President.

Gutierrez faces him, surprised. He assumed he would be privy to the meeting.

"Mr. President." Gutierrez bitterly walks to the door.

"Enjoy your drink, Mr. Promise." he says closing the door behind him.

"You look well, Mr. President," I say with a grin. He knows what I'm referring to.

"Please, call me Ruiz." he chuckles pouring, "that was quite a mess. One you fixed." He looks up with the bottle still in hand. "I'm thankful. I imagine you came here for a reason. My cabinet has been avoiding me. Several have resigned." He finishes pouring, swirls the glass and takes a sip.

He seems relieved to talk. A man with pent-up thoughts looking for a trustworthy ear. Behind his pleasant demeanor and dark circles beneath his eyes, concern. He's a smart man and I can feel his heart for his country. He's not sitting here eating a fatted calf while his country burns. He's thinking. He lowered his guards when the door shut. The best way to handle him is to be straightforward and honest.

"Why have you refused to speak with the President?" I ask crossing my leg.

The President stops and puts his glass down." His eyes widen.

"Where have you heard this?" The President asks.

"Didn't you?" I ask, puzzled.

"No. Why would I?"

"The embassy bombing is one issue. The other, seems of greater concern. The President has demanded the release and return of the twenty-seven missing Americans immediately." I say watching his response closely.

We spoke at depth. Thirty minutes pass quickly. We walk out of the private sitting room. Gutierrez is still standing in the hall speaking to someone. We shake hands; he returns to the room, and the door is closed behind him.
Gutierrez is to talk to me. He can't help it. I know he can't. He'll wait until we're out of listening distance of the President's door. Waiting for the elevator, here he comes.

"Mr. Promise." Says Gutierrez.

I turn to him as if I didn't expect him.

"Yes, Mr..." I say.

"Gutierrez."

"Yes. What's up?" I say intentionally casual.

People like him thrive on respect and pomp. I just can't feed it to him. You earn respect. However, he seems to have the trust of President Ruiz. The President wouldn't entertain the possibility of Gutierrez being disloyal. I didn't push it.

"The President's well-being is top priority to me. Do I need to be alert of anything... specific? I may be of some... well, service to you."

I look around to make sure we are alone. The guard is in the distance, out of ear-shot.

"This stays between us."

"Of course." Gutierrez leans in.

"The President is concerned-" I begin.

"All those people out there waiting to break in the doors-" says Gutierrez.

His already small eyes, squint.

"-No. The President of the United States is concerned."

Gutierrez looks like an eagle with a piece of meat in his teeth. Inside information is a tasty morsel. More than he thought he'd get. I'm spoon-feeding.

"He's concerned and ready to take extreme measures against Mexico for the bombing of the embassy. There are dead Embassy workers in there. That can't go unanswered."

"Rebels! It must have been. We would never-"

"Nevertheless, this could be prevented if the kidnapped Americans are released immediately."

The crease in Gutierrez brow deepens. He walks back and forward in this small hall, his stiff shoes clump with each step on the tile. He lifts his swinging pocket watch, then clasps his hands behind his back again. He's almost bursting with anxiety.

"When? How many days has your President given us?" He asks.

"Not days. Hours." I say.

"What! How could he possibly expect this?" His eyes widen.

"I forgot to give this to the President. It's the list of names of abducted American citizens. Would you give it to him?"

"I will." He takes it, looking at the folded paper thoughtfully. That's my job." He says.

Then I feel his hand on my shoulder. I face him again.

"Mr. Promise, is there any way you can ask for more time. Our police force is overwhelmed right now. We have no reason to keep your people. If we had them, surely, President Ruiz would do everything we could to find them."

"Just a messenger. Before sunrise." I say leaving.

I have planted the seed.   I get on the elevator. I am glad I spoke with the President.   The doors open in the tunnel. My phone rings. I didn't think I could get reception in this tunnel. It must not be as deep as I thought. It's Jason.

"There's a body," Jason says.

I stop walking. The tunnel guards stare. A sinking feeling in my stomach replaces hopeful momentum.

"Where?" I ask.

"Where Christian disappeared. Here are the details." Says Jason.

I look at my phone.

"I got it.   Heading there now."

I hang up the phone. After I go to view this body, I have another stop to make.   I know if I tell Jason he won't approve or agree. Who cares?

CHAPTER NINE

Tempest Bleu

I hate the dark. I have always hated the dark. The wall is smooth and cool. Finally. My finger bumps the light switch. I flip it gently and the light comes on in the room.

The room is bare. Tight woven immaculate commercial carpet from wall to wall. Sparsely furnished, there are a few stacked chairs, a plastic emergency evacuation route plaque on the wall. It's about ten by ten. A perfect box. The walls are pale blue, and the lighting is florescent mounted high, flush to the ceiling. The back wall has what appears to be cabinetry, but if Christian is right, and he always is, there is much more than that behind those panels.

"Electricity? How?" asks Jeff quietly.

"Panic rooms run on separate generators." I slide my back down the wall to a seated position and stretch my legs straight out and let my shoes flop off of my swollen feet.

"Are you okay?" Jeff asks.

"Yes. I just need to catch my breath. Are you?"

"Yes." Jeff rubs the back of his neck. "Sorry about that back there."

"I have had about five melt-downs that you pulled me through. I owe you." I look around the room.

Ironic that I am sitting securely in something Christian builds. It exudes him. It makes me feel safe. It offers security and hope. That's what he did for me.

'Does for me'. I never want to speak of him in the past tense. Jeff is looking at me oddly. I must be showing my thoughts on my face.

"This is a safe place, Jeff. Panic rooms often run independently. "I push my hair back from my face. "There are security cameras in here too."

"Where? You said your husband told you about panic-rooms? How does he know so much?" asks Jeff unstacking chairs for us to sit on.

"He made... makes them." I say, swallowing my emotions. "If I'm right, the monitors are inside that cabinet. There is a separate communication line directly to the police. There should also be food, supplies, and medicine."

"Tempest, how long can we last in here?" he asks looking around the room.

"It depends. Well, food rations will last a long time, that's if I don't eat." I smile, dropping my head. "It's okay to laugh, Jeff. I can survive for months. Seriously." I smile, raising my head again.

He sits on a chair and rests the back of his head against the wall. Our breathing slows, and we are finally relaxing. It has been a long night.

"Don't do that." He says.

"Do what? Tell the truth?" I ask.

"Down yourself. You're a beautiful person, Tempest. You and your husband were the nicest people Nancy…" he swallows, "Nancy, and I met on this trip. You're kind. That's what matters. That's why I let you and only you in the room upstairs."

He stands and opens cabinet doors. He finds packaged food pulls some out and drops a stack on the floor in front of me, crosses his legs sits on the floor opposite me scooting forward as if we were around a campfire. He reads a package and hands it to me.

"Here. Chocolate granola crunch. Hang on to your teeth." He says.

"Wish the world saw things like you. Thanks." I say fiddling with the bar wrapper.

"I know what you mean. No one wanted me to marry Nancy. Called her 'just a waitress'. The key is, don't give them ammunition. They don't deserve it. If it wasn't for you, we wouldn't be in here."   We would still be upstairs holding our breath waiting for one of them to break down the door. I would probably have…"

I see him look down at his package. Time to change the subject.

"I wonder how many more people are still up there."   I bite the nutrition bar.

"No idea. All I know is we need to get out of here." Jeff says pulling his satellite phone out of his pocket and the charger from the other.   He plugs it into the outlet and after a few seconds, a tiny lightning bolt over the battery appears.   We sigh and smile hopefully.

"You need to eat something.   Go on."   Like a mother, I watch him until he bites the stiff bar.   He completely squeezes a bottle of water into his mouth and gulps it down. He eats like a teenager. That's funny because he's such a well-mannered young man, well-groomed.

"Was this a honeymoon for you?"   Jeff asks.

I swallow and think. Strange.   I usually feel self-conscious about eating around people, but not Jeff. The guilt is trying to come in.   It was easy to push the thoughts aside when we were running for our lives. Now, here they come.

"Yes, a second honeymoon.   Twenty-five years ago, I became Mrs. Tempest Bleu. We stayed here. This was our dream honeymoon. The best we could afford was that room on the first floor." I smile.

"Wait, Bleu? Of course. Your husband is Christian Bleu? The Christian Bleu, the secret-keeper. He's brilliant."

"He is." I force a smile. "Have you met him?"

"No, but my father has. Everyone in our circle has heard of him or worked with him. So that's how you know so much about panic rooms. What's happened, Tempest? Where is he?"

I look down at the bandaged cut on the back of my hand and the memory of the morning Christian was taken came flooding back to me. Everything.

One day earlier.

The Capture

The stiff seat is too small. They always are. The armrests are dig into my side, but I won't leave Christian's side to sit in the larger chair opposite us. The elevator music can't drown out the sound of a crying baby and dentist drill stopping then starting. My right hand fits perfectly around Christian's left forearm. His hand holding his left cheek. His eyes are still closed, though I wish he would open them, and he's ignoring the beads of sweat sliding down his temples.

I dab his forehead with his handkerchief gently looking up at the receptionist asking her with my eyes, 'is he next'? She looks down at the chart and calls someone else.

I'm grateful that the kind elderly taxi driver brought us here so quickly after dropping our bags at the hotel. This is the last place we expected to end up on our second honeymoon trip in Mexico but mid-flight, Christian's tooth began aching him and nothing helped this time.

I'm usually patient to a fault. Not now, not with him. He is not the type to go to a doctor in the United States, much less in a foreign country. The smell in a dentist's office is universal. The medical staff is professionally dressed, that's universal too. The patients all look like they would rather be somewhere else and the waiting room is packed to standing room only. That, too, universal.

"Mrs. Bleu," says a woman dressed in a skirt suit, "I'm the billing coordinator for visitors to our country, I have a few forms and questions for Mr. Christian Bleu, but... I thought it best if you could do it, that way he won't miss his turn." She whispers, leaning toward me discreetly.

I look at Christian with concern.

"I really don't want to leave him. Can we do it afterward? Together?" I ask her.

Her eyes soft and she's wearing a pearl broach in her neck scarf and stockings despite the heat. She is in high-heel shoes.

"I'm afraid not, these things must be handled before the doctor will examine him. It's because you are not residents of Mexico."

Reluctantly, I nod. I want nothing to delay him being treated.

"All right. Give me one moment."

I wipe his head one last time, stand, lean in and whisper in his ear.

"Sweat, heart, I'll be right back." I say knowing he has heard everything.

Even with his eyes closed, he is alert. He nods and touches my arm. His linen outfit perfect for the plane, but he looks very overdressed for the dentist's office. We both do. My flats are leather, but they are stiff bottoms and the top of my linen pants just brush my toes. My blouse is sticking to my camisole from sweating and I can't wait to take off this tummy toning girdle.

The commercial said, 'hours of long-lasting, comfortable support'. Goodness, they lied. I walk toward the receptionist's desk and the woman gently touches my elbow and guides me to the door leading out of the office and into the mall of bustling people.

I stop and look back just long enough to see the receptionist behind the desk stand. She's pregnant. She pauses and looks at me. But it was an awkward look. Almost fearful or remorseful. She broke her stare abruptly and went back to filing.

"This way, Mrs. Bleu. Sorry for the inconvenience, but my office is just two doors down. I handle all the international traveler's payment issues for the mall."

I am not used to going to a doctor's office inside a mall. Especially such a busy mall. The shops are teeming with people shopping with their children, people laughing and doing what you do at a mall.

"Here we are." She says turning into a short three-foot hall and opens a discreet door revealing a desk, two seats and lots of file cabinets. There are no windows, it's dim, and looks as though someone shoved a desk in a supply closet.

"Please have a seat. You see how important I am, they gave me an office that used to be a broom closet." She laughs.

I sit in the chair directly in front of her desk, my back is to the door. The door closes, and the room is silent. She plops in a leather chair behind the desk and hands me a clipboard with about ten papers on it and a pen attached to it swinging by a stretched-out rubber band.

"Must we do all of this now?" I ask, fanning the pages. "This is a small book. I assure you we can pay in cash."

"It is not me, the doctor requires it, that's why he's still waiting. They won't say so, but they want assurance of payment, legal waivers, etc. My apologies, but the sooner we begin, the sooner I can take the forms to them and your husband will be examined." She says kindly.

"Okay." I exhale in frustration, jostling to grab the dangling pen.

There is no clock on the wall but question after detailed question and I declare I do not understand how some questions are even relevant, but I'm the visitor and must behave accordingly. Page two. I'm fiddling in my bag to find our insurance cards.

"You know what," she says, her eyes soft and kind, "you are trying so hard, I don't want your husband to suffer. I will call them, tell them you are with me so they can take him."

"Oh, thank you." I exhale and feel my shoulders relax.

"Hello, Elsa? Yes, it's me. I have Mrs. Bleu. She is filling out her husband's forms right now... yes, of course... she is moving as quickly as she can. Please make sure the doctor sees him as soon as possible, all right? Great. Thank you." She hangs up the phone and smiles.

"The doctor is finishing with a patient and they will be ready to see him.   So, relax."

"Oh, thank you so much."

"So, please, take your time, no need to rush, they will take care of him."   She shuffles papers on her desk and checking off items.

"Wonderful."

I wipe perspiration from my forehead.   My hair is sticking to my neck and face.   I'm sure my makeup is practically non-existent.

I know I don't have to rush, but I want to.   I want to be with Christian.   We are rarely separated especially in a foreign country.   I feel alone, although this lady is very kind.

I would feel better being with him.   Page five.   I glance around the room to give my eyes a break.   I don't want to stop writing to dig for my cell phone in my purse to check the time.   It has probably worked its way down to the bottom of the pit.

The pen stops writing.   I shake it and nothing.   She notices immediately and begins digging in drawer after drawer for another pen.   I feel my foot shaking anxiously.   Finally, she finds one.

"There you are, sorry about that."

She continues her writing but first glances at me,

sweating profusely.

It feels as if the air conditioning isn't even on, but it's probably my nerves. I'm anxious and this delay is upsetting.

"Would you like cold water? It feels like a sauna in here," she asks concerned.

"Yes, please, but not if it's a bother," I say wiping my head with my blouse sleeve.

"No, not at all. I apologize for the heat. I guess I've gotten used to it. I'll be right back."

She leaves, closing the door quietly behind her. A blast of cool air from the hall rushed in when she opened the door, but it vanished as soon as she closed it. I keep writing.

I feel like that child left sitting at the schoolmaster's desk after school has let out. I continue filling out the pages, flipping back and forward to make sure I have missed nothing.

Page nine. Something isn't right. How long has it been? Not just since I've been in here, but since she's been gone. I look around the office and realize something. It is odd.

I can't help but wonder, why give someone who is handling tourist finance for your business an office that looks as if a bunch of odd furniture was pushed in here randomly. Something else is very odd.

There is nothing personal of hers in here, nothing. No purse hanging on the coat hanger, no pictures, coffee cup.

Nothing.

I turn around and glance at the door behind me, it's still shut. I put the clipboard down on her desk, hold my purse to my stomach stand, and lean over to see the papers she was shuffling. She was looking over them so intently. I just assumed they were insurance forms.

I read one. My stomach sinks and I feel my hands go weak. They are random forms, mostly blank with large check marks where she just scribbled a check-mark. I lean further over the desk and my heart drops to my feet. The landline telephone that she was speaking into. The chord is dangling off the side of the desk. It is not even connected.

My heart begins to speed up I pull my papers off the clipboard, shove them into my purse and reach for the door. I will be horrified if the door is locked.

The cold steel doorknob turns easily in my palm and I pull it open. I exhale. But not for long. I pause for a moment because the thermostat in the room's corner catches my eye. It is off. What is this?

I want to get out of here, fast. I step into the small three-foot hallway and immediately I know something is deadly wrong. It is silent. It is dark. It is empty. The entire mall is empty. I teeter and feel my back touch the wall behind me, which probably kept me from falling straight to the floor. Am I awake? This doesn't feel real. But it is.

"Christian!" I scream, running toward the dentist's office.

My voice echoes in the empty mall and I can barely see where I am going. I feel the doorways and find the office. How is this possible? It's empty as well.

I pull on the metal door handle. It doesn't budge. The office wall is glass and there isn't a single glimmer of light inside. Everyone is gone.

My breathing is echoing in my ears and I push and pull on the door with all my might. What if they have him in the back on a table? Who would do this? Why? Christian would NEVER leave me. He would never.

There is a decorative door stop on the floor. It looks like steel. I pick it up. Yes, it is steel. I bang it on the glass above the lock on the door as hard as I can. The thick glass cracks.

I hit it again. It breaks the glass, leaving a hole big enough for me to fit my hand through.

"Christian! Are you in there!" I yell through the hole.

Nothing. I stick my hand in the hole to grab the lock.

"Ouch!"

The glass cut the back of my hand. I don't care. A click. The lock turns and I push the door open and rush in.

There, in the back. The examination rooms. The doors are all open. No one. Not a soul. And no sign of Christian.

I can barely breathe and feel things going gray. I stagger back to the seat. The seat where I last saw him. I sit gripping my purse in my lap, my body is cold and I'm shaking. Then someone touches me on the shoulder.

"Christian?" Relief, until I open my eyes that is.

"Senora?"   asks an older man.

He's a custodian. He's wearing a gray jumpsuit and holding a large bunch of keys.

"No!"   I weep.   "My husband... have you seen my husband.   He was here. Right here! Ta-tan outfit... I can't breathe."   The world is spinning.

"Lo Siento, Senora.   I sorry. No, speak English." He says.

"Call the police, please! La Policia".   I say.

"No, no Policia es en la ciudad. All Policia in the city." He says.

Before I realize what's happening, we are standing outside of the mall and he lifts his arm and a taxi stops. He opens the door for me. I get in and tell him the name of my hotel and close my eyes with my hand resting on my pounding heart while I gather my thoughts and pray.

I open my eyes and see the custodian waddling in his walk back into the mall.   All I can do is pray.

"Lord, let nothing happen to my Christian.   God, let him be in the hotel when I get there.   Please, Lord. Help me, I feel afraid."   I would have kept going, but loud yells and crowds of people break through my solace as the taxi pulls up to the hotel.

"What has happened?"   I ask the driver.

There are so many guests in front of the hotel, I can't see the entrance.   Some of them I recognize from the flight.

My Christian would fearlessly open this taxi door, step out, and extend his hand to me. He would pave the way, pushing through the crowd who usually would give no resistance, and he would get us to our destination. That's my Christian. That's what he would do if he were here. I must find him.

"Looks like your government did something." Says the driver comically.

I open the door, step out and am immediately pushed out of the taxi.   The person jumps in and yells, "to the airport and step on it!" The taxi takes off.

It is a war-zone. I clutch my purse to my belly and push my way two steps forward, then I am shoved backward so hard I almost fall.I feel tears well in my eyes.

"Excuse me… please!" I shove against the crowd.

I don't know what it is about Christian, but people stop and listen to him.   I'm the total opposite. They see me because they see him.   Without him, no one sees me.

I need to find him. I need an aggressiveness that I don't possess. This gentle, kind, Sunday school teaching, church-going woman hasn't had to battle for anything. But, right now, they are standing in my way of me getting to my Christian who may be waiting inside wondering what happened to me.

"GET OUT OF MY WAY!"   I yell and pierce

through the crowd to the desk.

My lioness roar wasn't as loud or effective as it felt, nevertheless was my best. Pitiful. But at least it got me to the front desk.

The attendants were bustling trying to explain things to the guests pressing their way forward. The front desk staff are returning passports held in the hotel safe upon check-in.

I'm being bumped and pushed. Oh dear, this isn't at all my element. Christian would probably bring calm to the chaos by addressing the entire crowd. He's not afraid to do things like that.

"Excuse me... pardon, I think you stepped on my foot... wait-" I raise my hand like a child in class trying to get the front desk clerk's attention.

"Bridgette? Bridgette!" I call to the front desk clerk. "Do you remember me? I'm Mrs. Bleu, you checked myself and my husband in just this morning. Do you remember me?" I ask her as she tucks her hair behind her ears and yells a response to a man behind me. She then beckons me forward.

"Mrs. Bleu, yes. I remember you. Your husband did not give us your passports." She says ignoring rude shouts of three other guests trying to get her attention.

"Yes, I know. Did you see him? Did Christian come here?" I ask, tears welling in my eyes as the words leave my lips. I'm gripping my purse so tightly I feel a few of my fake nails pop off and I'm hanging on her answer and feel I don't have the strength to hear the word, no.

"No, I didn't see him," I close my eyes and feel my bottom lip tremble. "but he doesn't have to come to the desk to get in the room. I gave you both key cards this morning. He may have gone straight to the room." She says.

That's right.

"Everyone! Please! Listen to me!" Bridgette yells to the crowd. "The United States Government has arranged bus transport for you back to the airport immediately. You can only take ONE bag. Leave the others, but this tag on the remaining luggage," she holds out a luggage tag with her fingers, "and we will ship it to you!" she addresses the crowd, myself included.

"When will they get here!" yells a man.

"I'm not leaving my luggage!" shouts a woman dripping in jewels.

"What about my refund? I paid in advance!" bellows another man surrounded by small children.

I ignore the chaos. I can't process it all right now. The only thing I know is that she's right. Christian wouldn't have to stop at the desk. Why are they trying to get us out of Mexico?

I do not understand what happened, nor do I care at this moment. All I want to do is find Christian and get home. Hugging my purse, I rush to the elevator. I feel like I'm dodging trees that won't budge from my path. Total chaos. The hotel staff is trying to keep everyone calm by handing out cold bottled water in the warm, crowded lobby. I press the elevator button up at least six times. I would run up the steps if I didn't know I would only make it one flight up before I had to stop. The elevator is taking forever to come. Finally, the doors open.

"I don't know where she is! Are you listening to me! Help me! You're the United States Embassy for crying-out-loud!" a man yells into his cell phone wearing a floral shirt walking out of the elevator.

He pauses and fixes his hair in a mirror beside the elevator. Odd. I feel my mouth drop open. 'Dear God, it's not just me?' Was it the rapture? Lord, no! Did I miss it?

"Sir?" I tap him on the shoulder. "Is your wife a Christian?" I ask, wide-eyed in a shaky voice.

He lowers the phone from his ear, his brow creases and he looks at me perplexed, then blurts his answer.

"What? That crazy bat? No way, she's the leader of an Atheist group. Hit her head one day and got up with a British accent. " He raises the phone again. "Hello? Are you still there? You better not have hung up on me... hello?" he says walking toward the front desk.

"Oh, thank you, Jesus!" I say out loud, resting my hands on my bosom. "It wasn't the rapture. I still have a chance." I step in the elevator, and the doors close.

The only thing that scares me more than being stuck here without Christian is thinking I missed the second coming of Jesus. The elevator is empty and quirky show music plays in this madness. All of those people in the lobby came from the rooms. I am the only one going up.

Forlorn, fear is inching up my back through the eerie silence of the hotel hall as I step from the elevator. Some room doors are left open. Garbage and small items litter the hall from the panicked exodus.

I'm looking for our number. I pull our key-card from my purse. Christian led the way to it the first time and I'm afraid, just like when he drives, I didn't pay much attention. I just followed.

Earlier, we rushed in and put our luggage down, freshened up a bit and left while the taxi waited to take us to the dentist's office. There it is.

Standing at the door, I'm bursting to rush into his arms. I can smell his cologne. He must be inside. I stick the key-card in roughly and it bends.

No. A small red light appears. Did I break it? I bang on the door.

"Christian?"

I turn over the card and push it in again. Something in me exhaled as the key card slipped in and I hear a little beep as the tiny light turns green.

I turn the knob to our suite and push. I step into the cool air-conditioning, the smell of fresh flowers and a waft of his cologne rushes up my nostrils. Strong, as if just sprayed. I inhale deeply, eyes closed, and exhale. The stress of the day falls from my shoulders.

He had the flowers delivered to the room before our arrival. He knows how much I love them.

"Christian?" I call-out toward the bedroom.

Standing in the living room, I walk through the open bedroom door just to the right and hear my purse hit the floor with a thud as I let it drop from my shoulder and rush into the bedroom. The empty bedroom.

I rush to the bathroom and his cologne bottle is open, just as we left it earlier. That was the reason for the strong scent. He's not here. Nor was he here. Everything is untouched.

A note. If he were here and left to find me, he would leave a note. A signal that he came through. I look all over the room. Nothing.

Everything is exactly as it was when we left. My emotions overwhelm me. The empty room is too much to bear. The weight of confusion crushes me.

What do I do? Wait here to just in case he comes here looking for me? Run through the streets like a madwoman looking for him?

Maybe I should go back to the mall. I was in such a frenzy, I could have missed something. I put my hands on my head and drop onto the bed and cry uncontrollably.

Time has slowed and I feel every second drag by and still don't hear the hotel door open, his singing, then "where's my calm water"?

Christian didn't call me Tempest. Tempest means a forceful storm, and he said I am nothing like that. When we were dating, I asked him what he liked about me and his answer stuck with me and became my nickname.

He said, "you're like calm water. Nothing stormy about you, dear." And thus, my nickname 'calm water,'.

But I don't feel calm right now. I feel a tempest brewing inside of me. I must get up. Christian wouldn't sit here and wait until I walked indoor. I won't leave him alone.

The United States Embassy. I need to talk to someone there. I go to the bathroom, wash my face and see spots of blood on my blouse. My hand is bleeding. There's nothing in the bathroom but washcloths. I need to tie something around the cut on my hand. I reach into my pocket to see if I have anything. I do. Christians handkerchief. The one I dabbed his forehead within the waiting room.

Tears fill my eyes immediately. I lift it to my nose, careful not to get tears on it, and take a deep breath. His cologne and the scent of his body fills my nostrils. I shut my eyes. I will not use this. won't wash it until he gets home. I push it back into my pocket.

In the directory beside the bed, I find the number to the U. S. Embassy and call. No answer. It's a recording. I'm not surprised they stopped answering the phone if some callers sounded like that man downstairs. I need to go there. I scribble the address on the hotel notepad, tear it, grab out passports from the hotel room safe and shove them into my purse. I take a deep breath, push my hair back with my fingers and go.

The embassy is the fort, I imagined. The streets are in chaos and I still don't know why, and I don't care. The only thing I care about is what has happened to my dear husband that I left in pain in a strange doctor's office's waiting room. What was I thinking? That was so stupid.

I pull my passport out after I step into the main gate and show it to the guard outside. I don't know if it is typical for them to be so heavily armed or if the hostile circumstances warranted it, but there are three guards outside with machine guns in their hands and they are in full tactical armor. The benefit of watching endless action movies with Christian during the winter months in Hampton, New York.

I can't wait to get back home... with him. Security is heavy. Finally, after waiting in a vast waiting room beside a sobbing woman for what felt like an hour, they call my name. I feel sorry for her and normally would have asked her what was wrong, but I couldn't bring myself to bare her story. I was trying to hold my composure so I could tell the account of what happened to Christian without bursting into tears.

An embassy agent who still has a gold-plated nameplate on his desk puts on his thick black glasses. His toupee moves when he turns his head. I try not to stare at the top of his head. There is a cold cup of coffee still full on his desk, and the cuffs of his white shirt are smeared from fresh ink. He's wearing a short sleeve dress shirt with a bow tie.

"Mrs...," he says, looking at my passport.

"Tempest, Mrs. Tempest Bleu. Mr. Douglass, my husband-" I begin.

"-First, Mrs. Bleu, you took a great chance coming here through these streets. One you shouldn't consider taking again."

"I understand. Mr. Douglas, my husband is missing." I say for the first time.

I didn't want to hear those words leave my lips. I expected a response from him. Any response. I thought he would be appalled and rush out of the room, tell one of those armed guards who would rush into the streets with a team and search for my dear Christian. That's what I expected. That's not what I got.

"How long?" he asks casually.

"I-I'm not sure... about three hours, maybe less. We were in the dentist's office for his tooth-" I feel my grip tighten on my purse that's in my lap.

He exhales, puts his pen down and leans back in his chair and takes off his glasses. The toupee moves back into place.

"Mrs. Bleu, I don't mean to cut you off but was your husband confronted with a threat?"

"No."

"Was there anyone in Mexico that approached you or gave you or him a reason to believe that they would harm him?"

"No."

"You say you were both in a dentist office?" he asks.

"Yes. In the mall."

"The mall." He leans forward and jots something down on a form.

"Yes."

"Which mall?"

"I..." my mouth falls open and I feel a blank look come upon my face. I didn't pay attention. That's what I usually do when I am with Christian. I don't pay attention. "I'm not sure, but it... is... big. A woman came to the waiting area and got me to fill out forms and when we were done, the mall was empty," I feel my breath shortening as I speak, "everyone was gone including my husband."

"What was the name of the dentist?" he preps his pen to write.

"I don't know," I mumble, feeling hope slipping.

I didn't think of these facts. I don't know what I was thinking. I thought coming here would fix everything. I didn't realize that the scope of what they could do depended on what information I can offer.

"All right. You went to a mall you don't know, to a doctor that you don't know, and went to a room with a woman you don't know." He drops his pen on the form and sits back again into his chair.

"How long ago was this?"

"About an hour and a half." I take a deep breath.

"You just told me three hours."

"I did? It may have been. What does that matter!"

"The time matters. Accurate information matters."

He taps the desk with his pen and looks at me again pensively. I take Christian's passport out of my purse, open it to his picture, and push it in front of Mr. Douglas.

"This is my husband. His name is Christian. That's the only question you haven't asked me yet. Christian Bleu and he's a real person. A United States citizen who pays his taxes." I take a deep breath. I need to get this man to care about Christian. "I don't have the right answers for you, I wish I did, God knows I wish I did. Please find him. Something isn't right. Christian would NEVER leave me alone. Never. We've been married twenty-five years and-"

I pause, seeing his two hands lift and his eyes shut. He stops me kindly.

"Mrs. Bleu, I know your husband is a real person. I didn't ask his name because his last location is more important than his name. I will look for your husband with the same fever if he were the President of the United States or a street sweeper. It makes no difference to me. I care okay, you don't have to convince me. Here are the facts," he leans forward and picks up his pen pointing it as he speaks, "there is a political issue going on right now and it stretches the Mexican police just trying to maintain civil peace around the city. So, from my experience, I can't rely on fresh intelligence coming from them since this only happened about an hour and a half to three hours ago.

I will send his photo and name out to the local police and see if there is any feedback. I will also send it to the local hospitals.

The time frame you said the mall shut down is when the social outbreaks began and the police shut down large gathering areas and it's likely this 'big mall' you described fell under that jurisdiction for shut down protocol.

We also have to consider, you said your husband was in pain, yes?"

"Yes."

"It is possible that he had a medical emergency in his procedure and needed to be taken to the local hospital. That would be the dentist's protocol, especially since your husband is a U.S. citizen."

I feel myself exhale a bit. Hope. I feel I underestimated Mr. Douglas's grasp on the matter. I think he has a handle on the issue at least.

"Do you understand?"

"Yes." I nodded, wiping my face.

"Next," He says, "The United States has issued an evacuation order for all United States Citizens as a precaution. These political issues can get out of hand quickly and there is already an unusual amount of United States Citizens reported as missing. We expect this number will decrease in the next few hours.

Mostly, it's just that people get separated in the chaos and out of panic, family or friends report them as missing, so there is a lot of gray area right now.

The best place for you is, home. The United States,

home. I have your cell phone number and will call you as soon as I get any information from the police and hospitals."

"Wait, you want me to go… home to the United States?" I ask, surprised.

"Yes."

"No."

"Mrs. Bleu, I understand your reluctance but you need to understand the circumstances at hand. This city may very well become a war zone-"

"-I don't care!" Surprised at my aggressive interruption. "I'm not leaving Mexico without my husband, Sir. He would never leave without me."

He exhales in frustration, as if he were expecting my response. He probably heard it a million times.

"All right. I don't have time to argue with you about this. Go to your hotel. Think about it. Would your husband want you in harm's way? I will call you as soon as I hear anything. Also, I will send the local police to pay you a visit and speak with you. They have good guys on their force." He stands, walks to the door and holds it open.

I recall the feeling of the cold arm of fear wrapping around my shoulders as I stood from the chair to leave.

Present Day

Jeff leans forward and puts his hand on top of mine. My eyes lift to his with tears flowing down my cheeks.

"Tempest, I'm sorry. I had no idea. All this time you said nothing. You just put up with me feeling sorry for myself." Says Jeff.

"You were going through your own pain. Besides, without you, I think I would have fallen apart already." I blow my nose. Loud. Hard. "I'm not strong, Jeff. Not really. I'm lost without him. I have never been on my own."

"Well, we need to get out of here so we can find Christian. You're stronger than you think. No more negative talk, all right?" He smiles at me.

"All right." He stands and looks at the charging phone.

"I'll get word to my father we are still alive, I'm sure he'll get us out of here. Still charging, good. Let's see, what do we have here?" He opens cabinet doors.

The smaller cabinet has food, vacuum-sealed packages and water. Another cabinet is a medicine. Another, a gun and walkie talkies and electronic gadgets. We look at each other and Jeff takes the gun quickly. He loads the clip inside but doesn't put one in the barrel.

"Hope we don't need it, but hey, glad it's here." He shoves it in the back of his pants.

He opens the two large cabinet doors and there are

monitors, a series of them.

"Tempest, look."

I stand and sit in a seat he places at the monitor console. Wide-eyed, we press a button and the monitors turn on with security cameras showing every inch of the lobby of the hotel and flash to the upstairs hallways. One camera shows the roof.

"Look, there-" Jeff says. "Can you go back?"

"Yes, they work on a cycle but there is a way to stay on one camera. Where is it... there?" I press a button and the camera freezes on the roof. I exhale.
It's the building's generator. It's on the roof. That would mean walking up the stairwell, fifteen flights, no elevator using the same stairwells as the bad guys. Impossible. Well, maybe not. No, is impossible."

A phone rings. We jump. My heart is in my throat. We look around the room desperately for the faint ring. Is it a phone someone left in a cabinet? Can the gunman in the office hear it? Jeff searches frantically.
I look at the monitor and the camera shows them sitting with legs crossed on the desk. I press the button, stopping the cameras from cycling.
The ringing phone isn't in here. It's the front desk counter phone. I tap Jeff. We look at the monitor and watch one gunman leaves the room to and answer the front desk telephone. We can't hear him, but we can see him.

"It looks like another person, upstairs. They're

going." Jeff says.

He lifts his fist to hit the wall and stops himself. He knows someone is about to suffer the same fate as his wife.

We both know what that means. That person is going to being taken or even killed if they find no use for them. We both feel anger and somewhat empowered by knowledge and the gun.

We could stay here. We may be safe until this all blows over, but there are people stuck up there who do not understand what's going on. They call the front desk for help and find themselves, victims.

If we get the generator on, the doors will lock and that means time for them too, but we would have to risk our lives to help them. It gives them time. Safety behind locked doors. To live until maybe the police come. Jeff is thinking the same thing. I see it in his darting eyes.

"What stops them from taking out the back-up generator once we turn it on?" Jeff asks.

"Nothing," I say with my fingers resting on the desk.

Jeff paces the floor. I look at the walkie talkies. Jeff looks at the satellite phone still charging. It has one cell so far.

"All right. So, we're doing this, aren't we? We have to agree one hundred percent." he asks.

"Yep." I can't believe I said that.

CHAPTER TEN

Caleb Promise

A motorbike. Compliments of my prior assailants. I tucked it behind the shrubs just before going into the building. In the dark, unlikely to be recognized. The wind on my face, the rumble of the motorbike's engine beneath me and the cover of darkness. Blowing through Mexican street to the location of the body.

Thick humidity that sticks my shirt to my skin. I'm sweating. My leather jacket flaps in the wind, but I won't take it off. Small groups of young men lock their eyes on me as soon as they hear the bike coming. Some walk holding pipes or have their hands resting at their sides. That is worst because they have a gun. Men hold a different look of confidence when armed.

Can I blame them? According to Jason's informant, they found a body in the basement of the shopping mall the morning after Christian Bleu went missing. I hope it isn't him, and I have an urgency to complete something else.

Maybe he resisted? There it is. The shopping mall. It is empty behind a locked eight-foot fence with barbed wire going around the perimeter. I park the motorbike and approach the mall.

I put my hand on the large steel lock threaded through a thick chain holding the gates together. It matches the description as the last place Christian Bleu went.

On the ground, a pipe. I wedge it in a loose link in the chain, and well, the easiest way in is the place of least resistance. I only part the gate enough to pass through. I don't want to draw visitors.

In the basement, down the service hall, the light from my cell phone illuminates a partially open supply closet. The smell of rotting death rushes seeps through the crack. It's a distinct odor.

I turn away to take a breath. I hate that I saw Christian's photo first. Him alive, smiling. Now, to see him like this. It's not the way you want to remember someone. And I cannot forget this.

Boots. Work boots on his feet. I don't think this is Christian. Unless they changed his attire to throw off authorities.

The body face down on the floor. One arm extended, the other behind his back with the shoulder dislocated. The head covered by a plastic tarp. I pull it back slowly. The crinkled sound of the tarp is the only sound heard. The mall is silent. Is it him?

"No."

I drape the tarp back over him, stand and exhale. This man is wearing a janitor's uniform. He has one wooden leg. I close the door and rest my palm on the closed door for a moment.   Not Christian Bleu, but no less important.

I read the mall directory. One dentist. One office. Easy to find.   It's upstairs. A noise. I'm not alone in here anymore. Yelling, glass breaking. I need to move quickly. Vandals are in an electronics store shoving cell phones into a duffel bag. There it is. The glass on the door broken, and the lock turned.

I fiddle through the days' patient files. Nothing. No file on Christian Bleu.   I didn't think so. Everything is as it was on that day, so it seems. From the looks of things, the office was closed in a hurry. They have cleaned nothing. Dirty instruments still lay in trays.   Garbage in the cans and the sign-in book still open on the desk.   They rip a page out. But it seems in haste, they ripped out the wrong page. There it is, in his handwriting. 'Christian Bleu'.

I walk past the office desks.   Nameplates.   Heading to the file cabinet, I stop.   Turn back to a receptionist's desk. Photos of a pregnant woman hugging a muscular man with piercing eyes and a serpent tattoo on his forearm. Congratulatory cards decorate the desk. A stack of invitations in pink envelopes with handwritten return addresses on all of them.

This capture was not spontaneous. But how? How could someone know he would have a toothache? How could they know the taxi would bring him here?

This office is upstairs with no elevator.   Christian Bleu is not the size of a man you can muscle through a place like this without drawing attention.   And toothache or not, his character is not the type to go quietly.

Standing in the center of this office, I can see the scene playing out. According to Jason, there is no record of anyone being taken by ambulance from here.   One last stop. There is only one thing I can think of that would make a man like Christian voluntarily go with captors. A threat. A threat to someone he loved. His wife. This man is smart. A business man. A negotiator. My guess, once inside the dentist's examination room, he negotiated. Her safety for his cooperation. That is the only reason Tempest Bleu is still alive.

Her removal from his presence was essential to their plot. Him not knowing that she was not taken, was irrelevant. All they had to do was make him think they took her. That's all they would need to get him to comply.

So why leave her alive? Why leave a trail? Why leave someone that would raise alarms to his disappearance? That answer is a little more complicated, however, I feel the answer will reveal itself as things unfold.

Finally found it. The security office on the first floor. There must be recordings from the day. I check. They have taken the disks. Nothing from that day at all. They don't know that we can retrieve all videos from the hard drive. There it is. Video from that day.

I watch intently. Shoppers walking by and out of the office. There they are. Tempest Bleu and Christian Bleu. When I see a couple, their relationship is obvious to me. I wonder if others can see it too. Whether a couple is bonded, happy, or emotionally separated. There, but not there. It is always obvious to me.

If they are bonded, it's seen in their walk, their eyes, their body language. In the brief clip of their exit from the stairwell and walk to the dentist's door, I see them.

She depends on him, even in his weakened state. He is leading; she is holding his arm, tightly. Her concerned brow. She loves him. His hand on top of hers, trying to comfort her though he is in pain, shows me he cares more for her than for himself.

They knew. Whoever took Christian knew. That's why they kept her alive. If they killed her, they would get nothing from this man. That means he is probably still alive. I want to help them. It's not just Jason's mission anymore. It's mine.

I fast forward. Tempest being led out with a woman somewhere behind the camera. Two minutes later... what is this? It's Christian. He's walking out of the office between the two men. Pause. One man is familiar.

The man with the tattoo on his forearm holding the pregnant woman in the picture on the desk. I memorized the address on the pink envelope. Fast forward.

The place is clearing out as if someone rang a bell. Fast forward further. There, Tempest running to the office banging on the door. I look away. Her anguish is reached through the video and grabs me.

She is running through the mall pulling on all the doors then circles back to the locked dentist office like a child running to its parent's side. I can see her chest heaving as she panics and tries to breathe. Leaning on the door having a panic attack. She sits in a seat in the dentist waiting room and a janitor limps in. That's the body in the basement. The pieces come together.

A lump forms in my throat. I know exactly what it feels to be left alone. Suddenly alone. I connect my phone and upload the video to my cell phone, then rewind it and let it play. It was her. Tempest. Every man's reason for cooperating with the enemy. Love. Wait, what was that?

Rewinding, they turn a corner, and there is no video camera down those halls. I switch to see exterior cameras.

Multiple cars pull out of the mall parking lot. The sun's glare on their windows make it impossible to see passengers.

Rewind. I lean in. There. Christian turned around and looked straight at the security camera and dropped something. What is that? I magnify the pixilated video. It's white. But the footage is grainy, and this machine is so old. I need to see it.

I turn off the video and wipe my prints from the console. If I feel, I can't think clearly. If I think clearly, I can win.

I go back to the dentist's office and walk Christian's path. It could have gotten kicked anywhere. I use my cell phone light and look down, walking slowly. I risk the light being seen by the vandals who have now increased in number, but it's a chance I have to take. There. Is that it?

Yes. White gauze packing for a tooth. I look further up the hall, another piece. A stairwell. This is the way they took him.

"You're brilliant, Christian," I say aloud.

Descending the stairwell, it ends at the underground parking garage I search the ground. There, about seven parking spaces away. Another piece. Black grease on it, but that's it.

"Well done, Mr. Bleu. I've got you from here." I mumble.

In my phone, I pull up the security footage isolating the parking lot and the car that pulled out. Its license plate isn't visible, but the color make, and model is clear. I need to update Jason even though I don't want to speak to him. I get to the motorbike. Whoever this woman is, she is a party to this plot.

"It's me. Talk." Says Jason.

"Not him," I say.

"Good." He exhales. "That means he's probably still alive. How did they get him out of there?"

"He walked."

"Walked?"

"Willingly," I say flatly.

"You think or know. And why would he do that?"

"I know. Security footage."

"This scene was untouched. Jason, no one came here. Everything is as it was that day. There is no evidence of an active investigation. Why?"

"What! I was told the embassy passed the information to the local authorities. I'm sure of that. Douglass wouldn't let that fall through the cracks. But, directly afterward, the protests started. Hard to say. We have no jurisdiction there. That makes you our eyes and ears."

Now, I'm wondering if he truly didn't know. The U.S.

wants to keep this quiet. I have questioned nothing Jason told me before, but the cunning way he led me into Wallie's life has me wondering about his motives and methods. One thing I know for certain, he needs me to get his wife home. He'll cooperate with me for that. For now.

There is an awkward pause that normally wouldn't exist in our conversations. Normally filled with a joke or kind comment.

"Caleb, I understand if you are angry with me- "

"-I'm losing time. I'll call you."

I disconnect. These people deserve to sit on a patio in their nineties holding hands. I can't abandon her. It's a feeling I know all too well.

Hopefully, the streets are clear with the curfew. If not, I must improvise. Besides, she may know something I can use to save her husband, but I'll need a safe place to take her if I find her. I don't trust the people in the Presidents' residence.

The motorbike starts easily. I pull a black and white bandanna out of my back- jean pocket and tie it around my neck loosely. This next move will require some anonymity.

CHAPTER ELEVEN

Tempest Bleu

We are going to do this. I am definitely not the superhero type. I'm the one the superhero rescues that's crying 'oh thank you... I don't know what I would have done if you didn't come'. The one in the grocery store line with that 'please be nice to me' smile on their face who lets people overtake them in line and says nothing about it.

I don't even correct someone if they pronounce my last name incorrectly, and I take the church volunteer jobs that no one else wants. Maybe I avoid confrontation because it usually ends with a fat joke or sneer. It's easier to just disappear into the background. To be that person in the room no one acknowledges. No attention is better than negative attention.

That's why I love Christian so. He sees something worth fighting for, although often, I don't. He would do this without thinking about it. He wouldn't sit here, safe, while people died. Here I am sweating bullets and I'm not even the one that's leaving the room. The risk-taker in this plan is Jeff. All I have to do is lock the door, so why am I so nervous?

I rub my sweaty palms on my thighs and study the rotation of the monitors to find the best path for Jeff. I want to talk him out of it. I feel safer with him here, but it's obvious that Jeff is my opposite. I see why Nancy married him. He's that guy in the group everyone wishes will look their way. He's a doer. Sitting in this room would probably make him crazy.

If I will talk some sense into him, this is the time to try. I couldn't bear watching on one of these monitors while they capture Jeff. He would fight, undoubtedly. They would have to kill Jeff because he would never give in. I can't watch that.

"Jeff."

"Yeah." He answers tossing a package on the floor.

"Maybe we should give this more time. Who knows, the police could be coming... could be on their way. This is a popular tourist area, they must be close and besides, as we said, nothing is stopping them from turning the generator off again."

"Yeah, but I was thinking about it. Once I get it up, you can use the landline to call for help. Besides," he kneels beside the pile of stuff, "I didn't want to worry you, but I can't get a signal in here. The satellite phone is charging, but it's useless... in here. The landline works but all lines are overloaded and calls can't get out."

I feel my heart sink to my stomach. I place my hand on my chest, and the cool of my wedding ring touches my skin.

"You should have told me, but I understand why you didn't."

"So, now you know, this is a rescue mission for us as much as it is for whoever is still up there." Says Jeff.

He pauses and rests on his knees.

"Tempest, as soon as we open that door, those guys are coming at us," he points at the door, "with the element of surprise on our side, I think I can get them before they get me. But even with this, he opens his hand, showing me a handful of bullets. "When I shoot, I don't know how many of them it will draw. No matter what, don't open this door." He pauses, looks at the floor, then up at me again. "If I get captured, I won't tell them about you or the panic room. You have my word. No matter what."

I believe him. Every word. There is no stopping him. I can tell by the look in his eye. It's the one Christian would get when he got his hands on a project that he believed in.

"Jeff, least resistance. That's the route we have to take. I've been fiddling with this thing and I think I've got it figured out. This panel is the main control for the hotel cameras. This controls the monitor out there in the office. When you get the power on, the monitors in that office will go on and they will see your every move. The good news is from here, I can freeze-frame their cameras. I'll lock their image in the hall when it's empty. They all look the same."

"Okay."

"We use the walkie-talkies, I will guide you. Use the earpiece to hear me. I've been counting. So far, it looks like about seven guys upstairs, plus these two give us nine. But outside in the front, those look like the transporters. Those men are bigger with bigger guns and there's about ten of them and three vehicles. Jeff, we are looking at about nineteen armed men after you and those are only the ones we can see."

Jeff stands. His mind is clicking. I know that look. Christian gets it when he works on a project that challenges him. Oh, how he loves a challenge.

The usual security cases were drafted and cookie cutter. Christian relished the moments when the client would come in and say something crazy like, 'I want my safe underwater with killer sharks circling it'.

"All right. That's good. I just need what... ten seconds to get to that stairwell, the one near the pool. Can you lock doors with that thing?"

"Yes. Only the security doors. Fireproof ones. Like the one on the roof." I smile.

"Nice." Jeff smiles. "Once I'm up there, you lock it down. I'll call for help." He shows me the phone, and sticks it in his pocket, "then, I'll get the generator up. I'll stay up there. As long as the power stays on, that door will stay locked and I'm good."

"What? Why? No. It's much safer if you come back down here. Why stay up there? The door is fireproofed, not bulletproof. All they have to do is shoot the locks, Jeff." I urge.

"Because I can have the advantage. One door. One way in and one way out. I can pluck them off. And, if they're up there, they won't be down here… near you. Besides, the longer the generator stays on, the more time people down there have."

Something sank in his eyes. He knows that this is a suicide mission. He knows it will be just a matter of time before the gunmen go to the roof. He knows the door won't hold and the bullets he has aren't enough.

"As soon as you get this thing on, they're coming up there for sure. They are not idiots. You can't get them all." I say.

"Maybe not, but with this," he holds up two grenades and an extra clip filled with bullets, "I can get most of them. Listen, Tempest, if things in here get crazy-"

"-You mean if they realize you're not working alone- "I say.

"-yes. If you see them come down from the roof, you get out of here. Do you hear me? Like you said, they're not idiots, they're likely to find this place too and you in it. While they're up there with me, you run and run far.

We don't know who we can trust, so don't go to the police. Call someone you trust. Do you hear me?" Jeff pleads.

Those are words Christian would have told me had he been here. Jeff's right. They could find this place. Now, I don't want him to go. He deserves to live too. Maybe he wants to be with Nancy.

"Say it Tempest, say you'll go."

Why did he say that? I can't lie. I won't lie.

"I'll go," I say, swallowing hard.

"When that phone rings again, they will leave. That's all the time I need."

I just sit here helplessly watching Jeff load his pockets with things and synchronizes our walkie talkies. He puts his volume on low and clips it to his belt and hands me mine. I spin my chair and face the control board. I clasp my hands to hide their shaking to do what I well. 'Lord, protect Jeff. Please, Lord, don't let him die.'
The front desk phone rings. We look at each other. This is it.

"You talk to me and just tell me where to go. You're my eyes, Tempest. I'm relying on you, all right?"

I nod my head. He needs that. He puts his hands on my shoulders.

"If all goes well," he says, "we leave here together. I'll pay for your movie on the flight home. Promise." He kisses me on the back of my head like a father would kiss his daughter leaving for college and goes to the door.

"Deal." I muster.

We look at the monitor for the front desk. Both gunmen are at the desk, but one doesn't have his rifle in hand. He must have left it in the office. One is speaking to whoever is on the phone. He smiles fiendishly, hangs up the phone and bumps his partner on the arm.

Jeff goes to the door, and I hear him taking deep breaths. Like an athlete. It's a diver's preparation. Force your lungs to fill with air to maximize oxygen content. Do this three-to-four-times, then dive. It helps regulate heart rate, especially in panic. He puts his hand on the release panel.

"In three," I say. The gunmen walk over the bodies heading to the center of the lobby, "two..." they go toward the stairwell Jeff and I used, "one. Go." I say.

Jeff presses the panel. The door to the panic room pops open and Jeff rushes out. He shuts the panic room door behind him. I hear the click of the pressure plate reset. I glue my eyes on monitors, shifting back and forward. He is in the closet.

"You are clear," I say.

Jeff exits the closet, closing the door behind him. My heart is pounding so quickly I can hardly breathe. Deep breaths.

The cameras are rotating. Where is Jeff? I must have hit a switch accidentally. I press it again. Fixed. I breathe. Now, I can control what I see. Jeff is almost to the stairwell. What's this? He didn't take the rifle! Why? Dear God, why didn't he take it?

Of course. He didn't want to raise their suspicions and draw attention to the office. Maybe he felt it would slow him down? Jeff is moving so quickly. I have to look ahead of his path. He doesn't afford me much time to warn him. The stairwell looks clear.

"Jeff," I whisper, "all clear."

He's locked in his mission running up the steps taking them two by two. His arms bent in running form. I can't help but feel scared for him. A door one floor above Jeff just opened. At his rate, he will run right into him. I flip a switch to check the hall camera to see if the hall on Jeff's floor is clear.

"Jeff! Stop! Step in the hall. Now!"

I watch him freeze, mid-step. The man opens the stairwell door. He walks down the stairwell. Jeff silently descends one step at a time. I hold my breath. The man pauses to light a cigarette.
Jeff silently pulls the door handle and slips to the hall, closing the door quietly behind him. He's in the open. There is no movement on that floor. But still. I could have missed something, or someone could just step out of a room. The man strolls down the stairwell, passing Jeff's door, he stops. Jeff looks at the security camera in the hall,

199

purposely knowing I'm watching.

"He's on the other side," I say.

Jeff puts his hand on his gun behind his back. He can't. not yet. He's only seven flights up. He has ten more to go. I can't see into rooms. If I send him into one, he could walk into a room filled with gunmen.

Wait. Beside him is an opening. What does that sign say? I zoom in with the camera. "Ice".

"Jeff, behind you. The vending area."

I watch him turn around and slip into the vending area just as the man steps through the stairwell door, onto Jeff's floor. He looks down the hall in both directions.   Did he hear him?

He approaches the vending area, pauses, then goes into the room beside it. The room I would have sent Jeff into.   I watch the door shut behind him. The hall is clear. The stairwell is clear.

"Hall clear, stairwell, clear. Go quietly. He's in the room beside you."

Jeff nods. He's in the stairwell again, ascending the steps quickly. I exhale. The stairwell is dark and Jeff can't use a light. He's feeling the turn of the stairwell by the rail and counting the steps under his breath. I can hear him restart his count on each turn.

To his advantage, the cameras have infrared capabilities, so the darkness doesn't hinder me. But it puts Jeff somewhat at a disadvantage. What was that? I heard something. Faint, but definitely a noise. It sounds like someone is in the office. Suddenly, I'm afraid to breathe.

I switch one monitor to show the office. I have to stay focused on Jeff. One of the armed men returned. What is he doing? He is going into the closet. Why? Why would he do that?

Dear Lord, what if he accidentally hits the pressure plate! I hear bumping around on the door. He's hitting the back wall of the closet which is the door to my panic room. A loud bang. I gasp loudly.

He stops moving. Oh, no. Did he hear me? He couldn't have. He's rubbing his hand on the wall of the closet and knocks on it as if trying to find a beam.

God, if he hears a difference in the wall from empty sheetrock to steel, he'll know. He'll know there's a room in here. He backs out of the closet holding a bottle of whiskey by the neck high, like a prize. I exhale.

"Ah, mi amour!" he kisses the bottle.

He plops down in the chair and opens the bottle. I exhale. I have never been so scared in my life. I wipe my palms on my thighs.

I am whispering, hoping Jeff can hear me but afraid the gunman will too. This room is supposed to be soundproof, but I wonder since my husband didn't build this one.

"Jeff?" I turn back to the panel quickly.

How could I have let myself be so distracted? Where is

he? Oh God, he is relying on me. There he is.

"I'm here. Top floor." He says breathing heavily. "Which way?"

I rush to find his hallway on the cameras. I got him.

"Turn right, at the end of the hall. Then left down a short hall. There should be up a short stairwell."

Jeff strides then, he stops. He must hear something. Something I don't see. He points to the right. I switch to the other camera. He's right. A man came out of a room down the only hall leading to the stairwell. Jeff had about five feet before he would have turned right. If he did, man would surely have seen him.

"One a man in the hall."

"A guest?" he asks.

"I can't tell. Just in case, there is a supply closet behind you."

"We don't have time to hide anymore. It's one guy? I can take him."

"No Jeff. Be smart. Just wait one moment."

Reluctant, Jeff enters the storage closet and shuts the door. The man looks toward Jeff's direction. Did he hear him? He turns to light a cigarette. There's a gun in the small of his back. He's no guest. He has no shirt on, and his pants unbuttoned.

"Tempest, there's no time. I'm so close. I can take him if he's alone."

"Least resistance, Jeff. Wait. He has a gun. Just give me one moment."

"I'm done waiting. These bastards killed Nancy!" he opens the door.

Chin down, Jeff angrily approaches the end of his corridor. Pulls out his gun, aims it turning the corner. I shut my eyes for two seconds and say the fastest prayer ever. "Help, Jeff."
I open my eyes and a girl in a man's dress shirt comes out of the room and kisses him passionately. He flicks his cigarette onto the floor as she holds his face in her hands. Her red nail polish shining.
He submits and they go back into the room. He never saw Jeff to his right. Their shadows disappear behind the closing door.

"God is with you. But you do that again and I'll kill you myself," I say.

Jeff looks into the camera at the end of the hall and nods. He had a burst of rage. He is entitled to that.

In the office, the other robber has returned. He's angry. He slaps his partners feet off the desk. The whiskey he is drinking splashes on his shirt. Sitting up, the partner ignores his anger and turns up the bottle to his mouth again. Enraged, the other snatches the whiskey bottle from his hand.   This is not good. He grabs it back.

Jeff gets to the end of the hall and turns left into the short hall leading to the roof stairwell. He made it, he's at the roof door. I exhale and rub my palms on my pants again to dry them.

"There are warning signs all over this thing.   Will it go off if I open it?"   Jeff whispers.

"I don't know," I respond. "It could be a silent alarm for the fire department, but we just can't tell. There's a green dot next to it.   That means it's secured. What do the signs say?"

"I don't speak Spanish."   He says strained his whisper, looking at the camera above his head.

I can see Jeff, but not the door.   Wait. Two armed men are going toward the room that the couple is in. If this alarm sounds, it will only take them seconds to be at that door. Jeff won't have time to make his phone call or fix the generator. Out of options. Either he risks passing that door to return to the panic room, or he pushes that door open.

"Two more men just went in that room.   What should we do?"   I say wide-eyed.

This is it. He comes back or dies there. If the alarm sounds, he won't be able to get that generator running before they get to him and I can't secure the door. Jeff would be trapped on the roof with three armed men and all the others that will no doubt come running.

Jeff answers in his way. He looks straight at the camera and pushes the door. He hurries onto the roof and shuts the door. I inhale. I can't hear anything until he presses his talk button on his walkie. I can't tell if the alarm has sounded. He's moving so quickly. Is it because the alarm is blaring?

I look at the hall, no one is coming out of the room. Jeff is standing beneath the outdoor camera. He looks up at the camera and gives me a thumbs up and a daring smile. I exhale, lean my head back and rub my stiff neck.

"Like a superhero." He says pressing the walkie.

Jeff pauses and takes a deep breath. His hair blows in the breeze. Outside. Not safe, but outside. We have been prisoners in here. It's dark outside, but there is a light above the door illuminating him beneath the camera and he's standing right under it.

"It's beautiful up here, Tempest." He takes a deep breath. Refocusing he looks around. "Right. There it is." He says running toward something.

It is out of range of the camera. I can't see him. Shortly afterward, he ambles back to the camera. What's wrong? He kicks something on the ground.

"This cage is locked. Damn!" He takes out the gun and looks at it.

They locked the generator. Why wouldn't it be?

"I got a signal. I'm calling for help. Then, I will shoot that lock."

It's so dark, I can't see anything on the roof. If it were not for the battery-operated roof light, I wouldn't be able to see Jeff. I switch glance at the monitor for the office.

Are they? Yes, they are fighting. Fighting over the whiskey. The guy that found the bottle is bigger, but the other, smarter. No!

The leader pulls out a gun and they are tussling. I hear it! It went off. The gunshot the wall of the panic room I'm in. I glance at Jeff; he is speaking to someone on the phone. It worked! I need him focused on his task, not distracted by what's happening here.

"Tempest. I got through! My father is sending help again. We will be saved."

"That's great. What about the generator?"

Jeff holds up a key.

"Found it near the cage. Genius's. Starting it now."

I hear the buzz of electricity flowing through the walls. The power comes up, the monitors in the office come on. Fighting, they don't notice the monitors turn on. I freeze-frame the locking the rotation. The men in the office look puzzled. I'm hoping they don't leave. Strangely. It's me or Jeff.

"It worked. Power is on. Great job." I say. "You need to get out of there."

"On my way." says Jeff.

"Jeff. You can't come back here." I swallow. " They are in the office. Get out."

Jeff looks up at the camera. His brain is clicking. He looks at his gun.

"Don't even think about it, Jeff. Not with these two."

Another gunshot rings out before I release the talk button he can't hear it. This time it penetrated the sheetrock and hit the metal plate of the panic room. The sound of a loud ping obvious to me and from the expression on the faces of the armed men on the other side of the wall, they heard it. I shut my eyes.

"Not an option, Tempest."

I pause. I am thinking about lying to him, but I am a terrible liar. I come up with a better idea. Besides, if I die, I don't want to go to hell. That scares me more than they do.

Jeff steps toward the door and puts his hand on the

knob.   He turns it.   I locked it. A lock that is controlled by me.

"Tempest, unlock the door." Jeff says firmly.

"Don't bother. It's okay. I'm safe."

They are picking the sheetrock back with their fingers where the bullet pierced it.

"If you're safe, unlock the door."

Jeff is smart.

"Move back."   says the smart one.

He aims the gun at the exposed steel and shoots three times.   I can't move. I feel tears roll down my face. It's only a matter of time.

"What's that sound? Answer me, Tempest!   Can you hear me?"

"They found me. They found the room."   I say wiping my cheeks.

Jeff grabs the doorknob and shakes it.

"Open it! Tempest! Open the door!" Jeff angrily points at the door.

"No, Jeff."

He takes the gun out and points it at the knob.

"Open it or I'll shoot it." He threatens.

My hands are trembling so hard I can barely press the talk button.

"You do that, you will die before you leave the floor, not to mention kill everyone in the building. Think, Jeff. "

He paces back and forward.

"Tempest. No... "Jeff silently shakes his head, looking into the camera.   "... not like this."

A sinking in the pit of my stomach. It was a good idea.

"They're breaking away the sheetrock. The other went somewhere."

"Can they get in? How much time do you have?" Jeff asks.

"Only if there is an exposed seam. There are seam where the steel panels meet. If they built the panic room right, the seams will be overlaid with stripping, possibly welded together. If they rushed, the metal panels are just screwed to the beams. That won't take long to breach."

The other guy returned. With a metal pipe. I won't tell Jeff, but they found a seam. I am watching my demise draw nigh.

"Tempest?"   Jeff says tenderly.

I hear the shift in his voice and I'm not ready to get sentimental.

"Are you still paying for the in-flight movie?"

I try to change the topic. They're prying between the sheets. Short cuts. They will be the end of us. My heart is skipping beats, but here, in this moment, I must find the strength to not let Jeff hear my fear.

"Yeah. It's on me." He says.

"You can get to the airstrip, Jeff."

I press the button quickly so he can't hear the metal being pried.

"That's not the plan. What are they doing? Jeff says suspiciously.

"I'm in a metal room with loads of food. I'm in heaven. Look. Things change. Get to the airstrip. That's a better plan. I'll clear your path, but you have to go now."

"No."

I have to get tough with him, or he'll come back here I know it.

"Do you want to kill us both? If you do, come back here, because I can't get these two idiots out of the room. You want us to live, get to that airstrip, Jeff. Now. I will only unlock this door if you promise to go get help. Go down the same stairwell. Say it! I promise!"

I must unlock his door now. That will give him a chance. Because if they find him there, he's trapped. I see the crowbar pierce the wall. They are through.

"Promise!" I yell.

"I promise." He says reluctantly.

I take the walkie and hide it and stick an earpiece in my ear so I can still hear and speak to him.

"I'll guide you as long as I can. If not, you're running blind." I say.

If they find it the walkie, they will know I'm not alone. I hit the button, releasing the lock of the roof door for Jeff, then lower light on the monitors and turn off the lights in the room. They are speaking Spanish and yelling at one another.

"Jeff!"

They still don't know I'm in here. I get on my hands and crawl beneath the hole they made and put my back against the wall, still able to see the monitors. No! The guys in the hotel room are running for the roof door. Jeff has his hand on the doorknob. I rush back to the console and hit the lock on his door, locking it again.

"Jeff. They are behind your door." I say breathlessly.

I back up into the corner, my back against the door again into the darkest corner of the room. The beam of light from the office shines through crack, widening by the moment in the dark panic-room.

My heart pounding. I shut my eyes and pray. I can hear a foot crunch debris on the floor inside the panic room. They slide through the opening. I only have a moment while their eyes have not adjusted to the dark yet.

They are in the room with me. They can't see me. They can't hear my pulse in my throat. The first one inside puts his gun on the console and touches the buttons for the monitors. He sees Jeff on the roof.

"The roof! The roof! "he yells.

No. They can't go to Jeff. Then what is that? Gunshots and an explosion outside. Then another explosion. It's Jeff. It must be. His grenades. He's drawing their attention. One turns to climb back through the hole. I rush forward a and grab his handgun he left by the console and pull the trigger. Again! Again! And again! My eyes close.

I hear the thump of their bodies hitting the floor. I'm still pointing the gun. My hands are not shaking. They are steady.

"El TECHO! THE ROOF, THE ROOF!" Yell the men outside.

The gun slides from my hands onto the floor. I'm a murderer. My breath returns. Jeff! He did it. A diversion. Get up, Tempest! I tell myself. Get up! I roll onto my hands and knees. Crawl to the desk past their bodies. My entire body is shaking. I feel cold. So cold, but sweat is dripping from my face. I pull myself up on the back of the chair. I stand. My knees feel weak. Wide-eyed, I search the monitors for Jeff.

Where is he? He's not under the camera. Is he still on the roof? He must be. I look at the monitors; the stairwells have armed men teaming up them headed to the roof. I find my voice.

"Jeff! JEFF! They are coming! Get off the roof!" I yell breathlessly.

Why isn't he answering me! They are coming up every stairwell. Most of them are past the fifth floor already. The stairwell on the East side is empty all the way up, but he's not answering me.

"Jeff! If you hear me, go down the East stairwell! Jeff!"

There he is! He's on the roof, just standing there. Why? What is he doing? They are one floor from the roof. The monitors outside show the vehicles are empty.

I grab a gun off of the body on the floor and put the strap around my neck. It's heavy. What am I doing? I'm on autopilot. My body is moving without consulting my brain.

I don't know how to use the gun. I'll do what I see them do in the movies. Finally, I see Jeff on the monitor backing toward the door. Why is he stopping? No. He glances up at the camera purposely. He's raising his hands in surrender.

"No!" I yell.

A pistol pointed at him. Then a shot. Jeff buckles over. Barely in view I see the shooter sticks the gun back in the back of his pants. He and two other men kick Jeff repeatedly. He must still be alive. I can't just sit here and watch this.

I run out of the panic-room and out of the office. I feel as if it's taking forever. The weight of the gun pulls on my neck and my breath is short, but all I can picture is them kicking him and punching Jeff. I envision someone kicking and punching Christian. He would do this for me. He saved my life with the explosions.

The elevator. Thank God for electricity! Finally, it stops on the top floor. I rush to the roof doorway. I can barely breathe, bustling with this big gun.

Through the door, I hear chaos on the roof. Grunts and groans. The sound of bones crunching. Dear God! They're beating him to death.

I prop the gun on my shoulder, just like in the movies. My hands are shaking, my eyes sting from perspiration. The room is spinning and I think I'm in the middle of a heart attack. It really doesn't matter now. Pounding. My heartbeats like a drum.

I take a deep breath like Jeff did in the panic room and shove my body against the door's metal plate. The wind catches the door, flings it open, I almost fall out onto the roof. Gravel crunches beneath my flats. I steady myself. The wind blows my hair upward into my eyes. And I'm blinded by the roof light and hair. I lift the gun. I force my eyes open.

"LEAVE HIM ALONE YOU BASTARDS!" I pull

the trigger, fanning the gun side to side.

A flat click. Nothing. By the grace of God, the heart attack will kill me before they do. I can't breathe. My heartbeat is coming through my chest.

I take my right hand off the gun and grab my head. Everything is going grey. A blurred figure is approaching me slowly with hands raised. An angel? I'm dying.

"Lord, I repent from every sin- "

"-Put it down, Tempest." A soft voice says.

"Lord? Is that you? I didn't mean to murder those bad men." I weep.

My body sways. My head is light. I take my left hand off the gun and wipe my eyes. Jeff slumped on the ground with his back against the cage of the generator. All the gunmen are laying on the roof. Some groaning, some look dead. Some twisted unnaturally. And the figure is not an angel. It's a man, a tall man in a leather jacket, standing there as calm as water. His deep blue eyes shoot straight through me despite my condition.

I feel my body fall, but he catches me.

CHAPTER TWELVE

Caleb Promise

The darkness wrapped itself around us, securing our escape. It's not a four-star hotel, but it's safe. A two-bedroom apartment above a bodega with a rear entrance is the best I could get at the last minute. I feel good about this.

Carlotta, long-haired beauty and the owner of the bodega, agreed on cash and secrecy. There is another feature to this apartment that made it very appealing. A secret ladder that descends from the apartment into the grocery stores storeroom. A good measure. I hope it won't be necessary.

Sitting in this creaky armchair with faded floral print, ripped and tattered, hearing the bathroom faucet drip reminds me how much things have changed in such a short amount of time.

The wallpaper is peeling and there's no door on the second bedroom. Some would cringe at this. Compared to my last lodgings, this is an upgrade. The flattened carpet is worn and musty. The black and white photos on the walls are random and there is no repetition of the same person in any two pictures.

It appears staged to seem inhabited by a little old lady, but no cookie-baking, kind-faced elderly woman is peeking her head out of this kitchen.

Carlotta undoubtedly is catering to those who need a secret ladder escape. It's worn but clean. Tempest is still asleep on the bed. We put her in the room with a door but left it open. Windowless, it's dark. I turned on the lamp on the night table so she wouldn't be frightened waking in a dark strange room. For someone with her wealth, this is far beneath her standards. I pulled the blanket over her like a taco. Inevitably, she fainted. It was probably better that she did. Jeff insisted we collect her suitcase from her hotel room and small purse from the panic room. At least when she wakes, she will see some familiar things. She snores.

Exactly as I expected her to be, real and caring. The breathing image I saw on the mall security camera. Still in the same clothes, too. I don't think I'll ever erase the sight of her bursting through that rooftop door.

I bought a bag of groceries from the bodega downstairs. Carlotta sold me some of her hand made tamales, the best I've ever tasted, and I ate my fair share from New York street vendors to know the difference. I bought some soda's in clear glass bottles, bright orange, a few bottles of water and turkey and cheese sandwiches.

It's quiet. I bite my sandwich and look at Jeff. He refused to go in a room. Insisted on staying on the sofa to watch me. That mission lasted a whole ten minutes. Then he slumped over on the soft sofa. He'll wake with a crick in his neck, but sorry, I don't tuck-in men.

I don't blame him. If I were in his position, don't think I'd trust anyone either. Is it that time? My phone rings.

"Yes. It's me." Says Jason.

"Any location on our target?" I say.

"None. Mexican police say they found nothing at the site. You have hours to find him. Caleb, if they lift bodies out of that embassy, the President will have no choice but to strike. Get President Ruiz to tell you where Christian is."

"What makes you think he knows?" I say chewing.

"The guy who sold Christian's itinerary talked. We know who he sold it to."   Says Jason.

I feel my teeth grit.

"Name."

"Gutierrez. President Ruiz's Personal Advisor." Says Jason.

This changes things. I need to create movement. Too many people would benefit from Christian's abduction. It's not even funny. His suspect list is ranges from the financially strapped to billionaires. Movement, that's what I need.

I expect the United States President will 'answer' back to an act of aggression quickly to appear strong. Too quickly, he looks hasty, rash. It feeds his base and strengthens his constituents, confidence in him. Destruction of U. S.

Property is one thing, U. S. Bodies are another.

"Who are you talking to?" Jeff wakes and asks me.

"Who is that?" asks Jason.

"None of your business," I say to Jason.

"Anything happening during this mission is my business. What's wrong with you?" Jason asks.

Typical Jason, accustomed to me complying. Oblivious that he changed the dynamic of our friendship? After all, he's an Agent, but he feels like my handler. This isn't what I want. I grew past being handled.

"I think it's my business." Says Jeff.

"Not you," I say looking at Jeff, "Relax, I'll be with you in a moment. All right?" I hold my hand up to him calmingly and bite a tamale.

"I'll call you back."

I hang up on Jason. Again. I pull it together again. My feelings about Jason's deceit almost got the best of the moment. Not here, not now. I want him to know he doesn't own this cannon. I fire at will.

Jeff is looking at me thoroughly. He's wearing a wedding ring.

"I appreciate you saving me on that roof. Who are

you?" asks Jeff, sitting up rubbing his neck.

"You're welcome. "I sip the soda. "How long before your father's plane lands?"

"Within the hour. Why?" He says looking at me suspiciously.

"Because I want you to take Tempest to the States. But, don't let her go home until I call you. Can you do that? No press. No police in the States." I ask.

"Yeah, yeah, I can. Listen, my wife, Nancy, they killed her. They dumped me at the hotel. I don't know if you can do this but, "he spins his wedding ring, "I want to bury her in the states. I don't know who you are or how you found us, but you think you could help find... her? I can pay you." he chokes back his tears and with a shaky hand, passes me a creased photo of her from his wallet.

His face bruised from their brief beating. A cut with dry blood on the top of his temple. I put the tamale down and wipe my hand on my blue jeans right thigh.

"I Promise, I'll do my best."

"Thank you. How much?"

"No charge." I say looking at the photograph and slip it into my pocket.

Between our eyes, I see he's a man who means what he says and trusts my word. His eyes skip down to the old scars on the back of my right hand.

I don't like being looked at that way. The way people look at you when they are trying to figure you out. I will do everything I can to get her body. I hated being stuck in that orphanage, unable to visit my parents' graves at will. He deserves to have a grave to visit.

"Thank you. I'm going to take a shower before Tempest gets up."

He stands tenderly, bracing himself on the shaky side table, and holds his ribs. I feel older than him. Never felt twenty-something. He's Ivy League. But a nice Ivy League. The bathroom door closes and the shower starts.

I press the remote, turn on the television, and glance at my watch. Stretching my legs straight out, they bump the oval wood coffee table and I cross my ankles. There are protests in the street in front of the United States Embassy in Mexico. Hundreds of people holding signs and marching with their cell phones lit holding them up in the air.

"Am I kidnapped?" asks Tempest, standing in the doorway with one hand behind her back.

"No." I hold my position and purposely look back at the television.

A statue of the Virgin Mary drops to the floor behind her back with a thud on the worn carpet. I look up at her.

"Sorry." She brushes her hair away from her face. "I was thinking of killing you."

"It's okay. You're not the first."

I have to wonder if she knows she said that out loud. I like her already. She finger-combs her hair, but it still looks tussled at shoulder length. Her top torn and dirty with some blood marks on it. The bottom of her trousers ripped, and she is wearing only one shoe. But her eyes. The kindest I've ever seen.

They are sad and swollen with gray flecks. Her thin lips, naturally pink, look as if they are smiling between her full cheeks. She's missing a few fake fingernails, but that's the least of her concerns.

"It's okay." I stand and walk up to her, extending my hand now that she is at ease. "We have sandwiches, soda-"

"You saved us. Who are you?" she asks.

"Mrs. Tempest Bleu, I'm Caleb Promise. I'm here to help you and to find your husband." She takes my hand and bursts into tears, holding it tighter and tighter as if it were a lifeline.

I lead her to the sofa and sit her down. I angle my flower chair to see her out the window and the television at the same time.

"I'm sorry, I seem to have been doing nothing but cry lately. Did I kill anyone? I remember holding a gun. Christian would be very disappointed if I killed someone. I'd go to hell for sure. Where's Jeff? Oh God, is he still on the roof?" Tempest rambles.

"Take a breath." I say. She inhales and exhales. "You're safe. Cry if you want to, okay." I soften my tone with her. "I don't think you killed anyone, but if you did, to protect yourself, God would probably understand. Jeff is in the bathroom. The roof, a thing of the past."

"Where is my husband, Mr. Promise?" wide-eyed.

"I don't know yet. I will find out. We'll get him home. Please, just call me Caleb. I'm just Caleb. "

"No one helped, Mr. Promise... Caleb. No one!" she stands angrily and starts pacing. "First, I called the Embassy, a man, nice man, Douglass something, told me he would issue a hunt and the local police would be investigating. He said police would come to my room soon. They never came. No one ever came." She takes a breath. "Christian would have been looking for me come hell, excuse my language, or high water. I was just so scared. Thank God they sent you to find me. Jeff and I would have died."

I can't bring myself to tell her that no one sent me for her.

"You did what you could."

"Your husband is a very important man, Tempest. Many people have reason to want him found-"

"-and many people have reason to want him dead. I'm not naïve, Mr. Caleb."

"Just, Caleb."

"Mr. Promise. Christian knows where people's secrets are kept. It's as good as knowing their secrets. People want to hide things and then want to make sure no one knows where they are. But on our second honeymoon. How dare they! You find him, Mr. Promise." She says.

"You think it's someone he did work for?"

"I don't know, I mean, that's the best explanation I can come up with."

I don't think she'll just resolve to calling me, Caleb. I'm not used to the whole mister thing, but I guess I'll get used to it. I lift my brown leather jacket by the collar off of the back of my chair. It's time to go.

"Tempest, your suitcase and purse are in the room. Shower, change. You'll be leaving within the hour with Jeff, back to the States. I've arranged secure transport to the airstrip and if you need it, your passport is still in your purse."

I look out the window. The smoke has stopped coming out of the embassy ruins a few blocks over. That's why I selected this place. I needed to see… everything. I glance at the television and translated words trail the bottom of the screen:

"BREAKING NEWS… United States military team is on its way to the embassy to investigate the nature of the explosion." The camera turns to a reporter on the streets of Mexico interviewing citizens protesting outside of the embassy.

"What do you think the Americans will do?" asks the reporter to a woman.

"I hope nothing. If it was an accident or something,… they will find out."

An agitated man behind her steps before the camera and yells:

"You know damn well they aren't coming here to talk. Even if it is an accident, they will smoke us to send a message around the world to not mess with their embassy's. Be real!" he steps back, joining chants.

Nueva Presidente! New President! Calling for President Ruiz to be taken over. Something isn't sitting right with me. In my gut, I feel as if Jason isn't telling me something which isn't new for him yet; I don't enjoy working in the dark. The newscaster continues.

"The United States Embassy was officially under the secure protocol, closed, gates locked, because of the rioting, however, it was believed that the eight Agency workers were still inside the Embassy. For safety reasons, they were advised not to go to their residences. The United States Ambassador was also inside the embassy at the time of the explosion.

How this explosion happened. We don't know. Mexican police and military are not permitted on-site as it is United States soil. All we can do is watch and wait for the U.S. investigation team to arrive.

Protesters have been saying we need a stronger President to handle issues just like this. This has inflamed the fire of protests that were seemingly burning down. The people are calling for a turn-over in power from the President immediately. Rumors say the people are in favor of Gutierrez, his loyal Personal Advisor."

Two things, I need to get inside that embassy before the U.S. team arrives and I need to get to Christian. I put on my brown leather jacket, zip it and head towards the door.

"Tempest, don't open this door for anyone. Your transport will call you on this," I hand her a cheap burner phone I bought in the store downstairs, "when it rings. Answer it. Say nothing. They will speak using the code word 'Bleu'."

Her mouth agape holds the phone but looking at me intently. She is afraid, naturally.

I smile at her and tap the lock on my way out for her to lock it behind me. I step into the hall facing the steep stairs in front of me. The stairwell is dark, but at the bottom of the steps is a wooden door that opens to the alley behind the store.

"Mr. Promise." She puts her hand on my shoulder. "Please bring my husband home. Everybody else disappointed me... please bring my Christian home."

The sincerity in her eyes sits in the pit of my stomach. I bite down. I need not know Tempest and Christian personally to feel the depth of their bond. It's in her eyes. I want to get them home. The last mission was for me. This one is about others, and it feels good.

I left Tempest in good hands. He's got integrity and I'm

confident they will get to the plane safely. It's time to spin the other part of this plan into action.

Going down the steps, I take out my phone and call the President of Mexico. Drop the pebble, create the ripple. The rest will play itself out naturally. He answers the phone.

"Still, no explanation for it…" the President says to someone else angrily as he answers the phone. "Caleb?"

"Mr. President, are you watching the news?" I get on my motorbike.

"I assure you that Mexico had nothing to do with this atrocity! Gutierrez, my Personal Adviser is here, and he assures me we have not removed our security from the embassy- "says the President of Mexico.

"Mr. President, please put me on speakerphone."

I hear a click then my voice echo's lightly.

"Go ahead." He says.

"This is all over the news in the United States news. Mr. President, you and I know, if this is no accident, the United States President's hands will be tied. They will force him to act aggressively, to satisfy them. Also, an explosion at the Embassy may be possible to explain, but fatalities… that won't go unanswered. We can only hope it killed none of the eight embassy workers. Did you get any information on that matter we discussed?"

"No. I don't know any Christian Bleu."

I shut my eyes and listen. Interesting. The President of the United States discussed Christian Bleu with the President of Mexico. I need to hear his heart.

"Mr. Gutierrez?"

A pause. I hear glasses clanking. He's pouring himself a drink. I know that sound.

"I am here, Mr. Promise. Your investigative team is arriving at the embassy within the hour. Our matters of state don't involve a missing person right now. The citizens of Mexico are in danger." Says Gutierrez.

"You didn't answer the question, Mr. Gutierrez. Do you know anything about the disappearance of Christian Bleu?" I ask.

"Impertinence. I answer to the President but to move past this triviality, no. That is your answer." Says Gutierrez.

Him, I did not believe. I hear a heavy glass slam on a table. Good, my fact-checker isn't broken.

"Your news is showing the people calling for a new President," I say. "I believe the rebels will use this opportunity. Mr. Gutierrez, just a suggestion. It may look better if you could be at the Embassy when the U. S. Troops arrive. The optics would help your President. It's too dangerous for the President to go personally." I say.

"He's right." Says President Ruiz. "Be at the sight waiting for them and speak to the reporters."

"Si, Presidente, I will leave now." Says Gutierrez.

I hear a door close and a pause of silence while the President listens. Then he speaks.

"That was a brilliant idea, Mr. Promise."

"I hope it works, Mr. President." We hang up.

I open the thick wood door and walk to my motorbike parked around the corner. The frenzy two blocks away has successfully cleared this block. Ensures the safety of my two hidden guests.

Fire trucks and newscasters dot the street. Flashing lights glow in the darkness between the buildings and people scurrying around with their cell phones aimed at the embassy, only a shell with the roof blown out.

It's almost dawn. If time permits, I want to get inside the embassy. I have a feeling about something, but I need to be sure.

The motorbike starts. I tie my bandanna across my face, covering my nose and mouth. Zip my brown trusty leather jacket and feel the heat of Mexico trapped inside my chest. This place is filled with passion and beauty. Passing these buildings, restaurants, and closed shops, against this deep dark sky full of stars, feels like a forgotten paradise.

There is a tremendous difference between this area and

where Tempest's hotel is. The hotel strip backs the beaches and is nothing short of breathtaking. Luxury from the time you step foot on the property backed by water for as far as I could see. But here, it's where the people who work in those hotels live. And it looks nothing like that.

The road turns from pavement to pot-hole filled streets to dirt road. The dust the bike is kicking up behind me forms a trail. There are open houses only three concrete walls, a roof and dirt floors open to the road. They sling a curtain up, which they probably close at night or during the rain. It is so hot. Tonight, their curtains are up and I can see people sleeping in hammocks and on wood crates on the floor covered by blankets.

This is the side of Mexico tourists don't see. A bicycle with cloudy water gallons tied to the handlebars and a scavenging stray dog is hunting for scraps while people sleep. As I roll by, heads lift. In this disguise, they are probably fearing the worst.

The address is near. A cluster of townhouses. I drive past the property and park the bike around the corner and walk toward the property. It looks abandoned. There are no lights. This is it.

CAPTURED

CHAPTER THIRTEEN

This is it. The address on the mail I found in the dentist's office desk. From the photo on her desk, she appears about six months pregnant. Boyfriend? Husband? Not sure, but he's one of the guys escorting Christian out of the dentist's office.

I walk around to the back alley behind the row of houses. A few cars are parked in the alley. I will need one. I use a knife to get into the car, pull the visor, no keys. Press my palm on the seat cover and there they are. Do people still really do this? Fortunately for me, they do.

I stick the keys in my jean pocket and walk to the back door silently. Three concrete steps lead to the door and there is a dim back-light above the door. Parted debris on path show several footsteps, and one set is dragged. Why would a cooperating man need to be dragged?

The basement door is a Dutch-door. One of the four windows cracked and coated by pieces of brown tape. I walk up the path a sound of a television grow louder. It is a soccer game. I step cautiously. Broken glass and debris on the floor. Blood. Not pooled, dripped, leading to the door. I drag my shoe over it. It's still wet. Old, but not dry. Whose is it? Christian's? We'll see.

I ascend the three concrete steps and peek in the window past the broken tape. I slow my breathing. My thoughts are clear and steady. One of the four panes of glass on the door is broken replaced with a piece of cardboard. Stained curtains hang from the door, flapping slightly from the breeze blowing through spaces between the cardboard and door.

A shadow passes the door. I duck. Dishes clank, placed in a sink, and the shuffle of a woman's slippers stop at the sink. There must be no carpet on the floor.

Water running and the clanking continues. No other voices. I peek through an opening in the curtain and there is a dark-haired woman at the sink with an apron tied high at her back. A man sits on a dingy, torn sofa with his back to the door watching television. Beside the television, a door with a large new lock on it. Christian. It must be. What else in a place like this would need to be locked inside a room?

Voices. I hear them coming, laughing and talking, but I can't see them. Where are they? Of course, coming down the basement steps from inside the house. I shut my eyes and listen. Two, three, five of them. Great. I open my eyes.

Insight, stocky men. They greet the seated man with respect. He's the leader. They take a beer from the rectangular coffee table and sit on the sofa and the odd chairs around the television.

The water turns off. Where is the woman washing dishes? She's not at the sink. I look down and feel the doorknob turn against my stomach.

There are no bushes beside the house to hide behind.

Nothing.   Nowhere to hide. The door opens.   The woman steps out, pauses, looking up at the unlit light bulb.   She stands on her tiptoes on the top step, trying to reach the bulb with a small bag of trash dangling in her left hand. She is pregnant. Very pregnant.

That's the benefit of being six foot two.   I reached up and turned the bulb, loosening it until it went off. I needed a shadow because I'm in it. Right beside her, a breath away.   Bent down beside the steps.   She teeters on her tiptoes with her loose dress swinging around her knees draped over her pregnant belly. The reason her apron is tied so high.

"Rico!"   she yells.

No, we don't want Rico.   Maybe it will benefit me, but that's not the plan.

"Que?"   Rico answers.

"La Luz!.   Fix da light!"   she yells.

I hear him get up and his footsteps approach the door. If he turns the bulb, they will both see me immediately.

"I told you it was going out two days ago!   Dos Dias y nada!   You do nothing."   She fusses.

Rico's shadow approaches it grows shorter as he gets to the door.   Then he stops and goes into the kitchen.

"Forget it!   You wanna start that again!   Cada dia the same thing every day! Telling me what I didn't do. Not tonight Maria."   Rico yells opening the fridge.

Glass bottles clank, and I hear a bottle cap bounce on the floor. I hear the creek of his seat. He must have sat down.

"You two, shut up! I can't hear the game." Yells a man.

"Do you mind? I'm having a private conversation with my precious wife." Rico says. "Run! Run! Run!" he cheers on a player.

"The light is out? Where?" asks the leader says concerned.

"Idiot. Forget it." She grumbles and carefully waddles down the steps a hand's length from me toward two metal garbage cans in the alley.

I stand quickly. My leather jacket brushes the house. I walk up the steps and glance behind me. The pregnant woman is still waddling toward the alley with the garbage bag swinging beside her. She must be furious. I can hear her grumbling in Spanish to herself. I step into the house and lock the door behind me. It's better if she's not in here for this.

No one looks up. They are engulfed in their game. Drinking beer and elbowing each other. Everyone except the leader. I look at the door with the lock positioned just behind him.

"They will lose," I say.

The others turn, startled by my male voice. My bandanna is still tied around my face, so they probably think I'm here to rob them. In seconds, four of them are on their feet. The one sitting. The leader.

His hair trimmed well. He sips his beer, eying me from head to toe. A mistake. One knife, three guns, and our leader is armed. Knife first. He throws it at my face. A side-step and it lodges in the door. I pull it, drop to one knee and hear the bullet whiz past where my head was. A flip of my wrist, the knife enters the knife throwers' chest in one smooth move. Vital organs spared.

Next, the man closest to me with a gun. I stand, step forward with my left leg, put my foot behind his and pull him toward me, gun arm extended. He pulls the trigger. Shoots the fridge. Another shot inevitable. I push down on his forearm. He shoots his knee. Dogs start barking outside.

He's my shield. Slumped, I turn him around. He releases the gun to grab his knee; I catch it. Pull his ankle gun and slide my hands beneath his arms. The other two men shoot. The bullets lodge in my shield's torso. His body goes limp.

I drop to one knee, going down behind his falling body. Two shots. One to each gunman's right shoulder. They drop their guns. Grab their arms. Rico curses at me as he grabs his shoulder. I stand.

That leaves one. The seated leader who has been drinking a beer through all this. My left gun, aimed at Rico who is calling me every name he can think of, my right, on the seated leader whose calmness impresses me.

The pregnant woman is pounding on the door. If not handled right, the leader will kill Rico, and I kill the leader starting a never-ending war. I don't need that. I won't leave that unborn baby fatherless.

Through the curtain, I can see the pregnant woman facing the door and pounding on it relentlessly, yelling for Rico. I adjust my aim at the seated leader and shoot the lock behind his head. He doesn't even blink. I put my gun's aim back on the leader. The deadbolt lock drops off.

"Open it," I say to Rico.

He doesn't move.

"I don't ask twice," I say to him.

Rico looks at the seated leader who nods. Hurriedly, Rico goes to the door, hand still on his shoulder. He pushes the door open with his foot.

It's empty. A set of bloody handcuffs dangle from the metal bed frame.

"Where." I ask.

"You're on the wrong side Gringo." Says the seated leader.

His voice raspy and deep. He lights a cigarette.

"Just want the package." I glance the room for clues. "My guess is, you've already been paid. You have nothing more to gain from this deal. Where did they take him?"

The leader puffs his cigarette, eyes on the ceiling. He never closes his eyes completely. Not even when he blinks.

Time is running out. He may stall for back up to come. I keep my right gun on the seated leader and turn my left gun to the door.

Directly at the pregnant woman yelling at the door.

"You know I won't miss," I say to Rico.

Rico sweats. He looks at the leader who says nothing. Blood streaming down Rico's fingers.

"He won't do it, Rico." Says the seated leader tapping his ashes onto the floor.

"He's crazy! He came in here with all of us, didn't he!" yells Rico.

"Don't lose it, Jeffe. Calmate, Rico." The seated leader says.

"It's not his baby, Rico." I cock my gun aimed at the door. "Tell me. I leave. You change that light bulb and finish watching your game."

She breaks the glass on the door near the lock and rips out the cardboard.

"If she comes in this room, I have to kill her. Talk." I say.

"They took him-"

"Silencio!" yells the seated leader.

"The church near the Emba-"

The seated leader pulls his gun. He's going for a head-shot. I pull my trigger. Rico drops to the floor. He yells.

"My foot! I hate you!" Rico yells.

The leader's shot misses when Rico drops.

"You were saying?" I say.

"The church... ah! The one near the U.S. Embassy! The basement." Replies Rico.

"You're a dead man, Rico. Un ratton." says the leader.

"How many?"

"I don't know! He's guarded. But, he's... he's...."

"He's what?" I say, looking at the door behind me.

The pregnant woman's hand is through the window fiddling around the lock.

"He's sick. His heart or something."

"Shut up."

"Forget you! You going to let him kill Maria and my baby! Tato is my cousin! Remember that. You're here because of him! You're the dead man!"

The leader sits back in his seat. There was truth in Rico's words.

"Rico, take her and go.   Now."

I lower my gun from the door but keep the other on the seated leader.

Rico unlocks the door and bustles Maria out the door.

"What happened? Rico! You're bleeding?"

"Let's go."

"Where are we going?"

"Shut up. You going to wake the whole neighborhood."

"Don't tell me to shut up…"

Their voices fade as they leave the house. I stand in the doorway and face the seated leader.

"You will find, all your men are wounded, but alive. I didn't wound their limbs."

"Bodies are a dime a dozen here." He says lighting

a cigarette.

In a flash, he aims and shoots the moaning shot man in the head. He could have shot me if he wanted to. So why am I still standing here?

"Who paid you to take him?"

"Why should I tell you anything? Because you came here and did this?" he waves his cigarette, smiling.

"It's a job for me. Just like for you. You will tell me because there may be another job for you. "

He laughs.

"True. It's a job, for me. I owe no one allegiance. I'm my own man. I run my show. How about you?"

Those words really resonate with me. I pull down my bandanna.

"A job." I say.

"No. That look of hope in your eye when the door was opening, gave you away. When it's just a job, you don't care. You don't care if people like Rico live or die."

"My guess. If you wanted to kill Rico, you would have. This Tato is why you didn't. If it is just a job for you, tell me. Who paid you?"

He crushes his cigarette in the full ashtray, crosses his

leg and half-blinks, then looks at me. His eyes cold as shark eyes. Flat. This man has killed people. Lots of them.

"Gutierrez.   Promised he'll be the next El Presidente.   Unlimited power and money for us."   He laughs.   "I don't know why I listened to him.   I think I was drunk when I made the deal."   He chuckles.

"A man that takes power will have it taken from him,"   I say.

"That's true.   Masked man, you want my power? The power to walk in rooms and be respected?   Then you have to not care."   he says, wincing one eye.

"I don't want your power," I say.

"You want a job, Gringo."   He jokes.

"No thanks, Pa-pa. I just want to get this guy home. But, I may have one for you."

He picks up a beer. We talk. He agrees.

"Rico is right." He sips it. "He's not doing good. Wasn't us. I don't deliver damaged goods."

"So, the bloody handcuffs are what?"

"Him trying to escape." He says.

It's time to go. I turn to the door and step over the threshold when I hear it. A pop. I'm shot.

I look down and see blood swelling on my right thigh. A hole in my jeans.

"We're even." He tosses the gun on the table. "Went straight through. No major arteries. Don't come back to Mexico, Gringo." He says siting back watching the soccer game.

He knows me showing him my face means I'm not scared of him. He respects that.

"Don't give me a reason to," I smirk.

Turning away walk to the car as normally as possible. A New York trademark, let no one know how much something hurt. I tie the bandanna around the wound. It burns. I need to get to the church before they move him again.

Something in me settled in. I feel as if I was made for this now. Somehow, the grime of that room didn't intimidate me because of what I lived through before. I don't know if this is good or not, but for now, I'll let it serve its purpose.

CHAPTER FOURTEEN

They barricade the street with the Embassy from vehicles entering. I leave it and walk toward the destroyed embassy building. A gaping hole in the roof. The explosion was powerful enough to blow out the windows of the buildings across the street and take down the perimeter security gate.

I need to look inside. My curiosity fueled by a gut feeling. Another newscaster arrives in front of the embassy. As soon as the camera lights turn on, the protesters crowd flocks to it. A skirmish draws the remaining United States Embassy guards to the front of the building. Part of the crowd spurt their support for President Ruiz behind the newscaster, others yell 'Nueve Presidente', 'new President', in Spanish. Now is the time to move.

I tighten the bandanna over the gunshot and slip into a broken window in the embassy's rear. Black suit-stained walls, glass crunches beneath my feet.

Even in the dark shell of the embassy, there is a pulse. The pulse of tension and uncertainty. It will only take three minutes to confirm or eliminate my suspicions. I descended the steps of the basement, lighting the way with my cell phone flashlight. Something snags the left sleeve of my leather jacket. A large steel beam lodged in the wall. I pull free, turn the corner and there it is. The vault-style door. Underground bunker and panic room for embassy personnel. They had no reason to open it. Frankly, they didn't need to. Hearing them arguing inside was enough proof of life.

   Back on the street now, I pass the media to get to the church where Christian is held. The lights from newscasters' cameras gather in one spot. Gutierrez. He will use this as his means to address the people of Mexico and declare his position. Whatever is in a man comes out in the spotlight.

He leaped at the stardom as imagined. I needed him to be visible, where he could be found once this is all over. I also needed President Ruiz to see for himself what a snake Gutierrez is. Shining light on a snake shows all his scales.

I fed him an offer he couldn't refuse. A platform in front of the cameras. As I told President Ruiz in our private meeting earlier, you don't sit and wait for a snake to slither out. You flush him out.

He will either state support of President Ruiz or declare himself the new President of Mexico. He took the President's security team with him, leaving President Ruiz's residence unguarded. Easy since they were used to seeing him give orders. So he thinks. I maneuver in the shadows past the cameras.

   "Vive Nueve Presidente Gutierrez!"   yells a protester.

A sea of voices joins the chant. No doubt, pre-planted by Gutierrez himself.

"I am honored to be offered this opportunity. People of Mexico. Hear me now. President Ruiz loves Mexico. He loves the people of Mexico. But, he has had his time! This," he lifts his arm toward the destroyed Embassy, "is what weak leadership got us. Now, we need to join against the United States! I accept your offer to be the new President of Mexico!" Gutierrez yells, throwing his arms up in the air. "Vive Mexico!"

By now, President Ruiz's residence is surrounded by Gutierrez's men who are being recorded by the security camera mounted on the outside of President Ruiz's private residence. Before I left the townhouse Christian was held in, I made a deal with the leader to ensure the safety of the President. He is not likely to fail. I paid him half of his price and will deliver on the other half. It is all business as far as he is concerned. I knew he wouldn't follow me to keep me from getting Christian. After all, they paid him to hold him, not to save him.

Right now, Ruiz is watching the news and has seen Gutierrez riding in like a savior on a white horse for all of Mexico to see. I can only imagine what he is calling him. I didn't learn those words in Spanish class.

The betrayal has sunk in. While Gutierrez is occupied shining in the spotlight, which was the plan all along, I move toward the church. Toward Christian. We're running out of time. If the U. S. Helicopters arrive before I get Christian. It's done.

I stop, close my eyes, and listen. Beyond the chanting, the glass shattering, I hear them like crazed wasp wings in the distance. Helicopters approaching. Christian is a pawn on the Gutierrez chessboard to capitalize on the money and influence of Christian's wealthy and powerful clientele. He would need it if he dethroned President Ruiz.

Cooperation from the rich and powerful are not free. He assumed to get it by force. A wise play to obtain resources. However, it only works if Christian is alive. I need to talk to Tempest. She may know something about his health condition that can help both of us. I call her. She should be on her way to the airstrip now.

"It's me," I say.

She answered the phone but didn't speak.   Smart lady.

"How do I know?"   she asks.

"I am keeping my Promise."

I hear her exhale.

"Do you have him? Is he all right?   What's going on?"   she rambles.

"Is that Caleb?"   I hear Jeff ask.

"Yes."   She says to Jeff.   "We are in the car, almost there."

"Good. Tempest, does he have a medical condition?"   I ask as calmly as possible.

The protesters are shoving and I can barely hear her

over their shouts.

"Hello? Caleb! I can't hear... Hello!" Tempest says.

"Yes! I can hear you. DOES HE HAVE A CONDITION?" I yell.

"YES! HIS HEART. HE TAKES TABLETS. Dear Lord! I should have given them to you! What was I thinking?" she says beginning to get hysterical.

"WHAT ARE THEY? TELL ME." I yell.

I place my finger over my opposite ear so I can hear her better. She tells me the medication and the dosage. I see a pharmacy a few buildings up. It was vandalized.

"GOT IT." I hang up the phone.

Guards are lingering on the church steps. They are President Ruiz's military who have turned.
My leg injury makes me limp. But it's what I hear behind me makes me stop in my tracks.
A United States fighter jets swoops above, scouting the area and serving as a warning. In the distance, a helicopter, a Black hawk. I move.

I run into a looted pharmacy, stepping over fallen shelves and glass crunched beneath my feet. The pharmacy is practically empty but by a miracle to find it. The medication is in syringe form. Perfect. I also grab a syringe of adrenaline and bandages, climb out of the broken storefront window, and run across the street toward the church. Only two guards are on the front doors of the church. The rear is more heavily protected.

"Excuse me. I'm lost. Can you tell me where the…"

A swift blow to the temple and the man drops. I pull his body behind a statue out of sight and have my gun on the other. I hit him with the butt of the gun, and he drops where the other one lays. The stone steps worn and dipped.   The large arched wooden plank doors creak. The doors have engraved crosses on each. I step inside and shut the door behind me.

The alter is concealed by a heavy clouded white plastic tarp hanging from the ceiling. Pews are missing and some are broken. A burst pipe drips from the ceiling, lending the only sound to the room.

The room is dusty, which is good.   I look down and the dust pattern, footsteps left in the dust lead me right to the where Christian is being held.   Boot marks and two shoes drag marks in the dust lead toward the alter and disappear behind the tarp. I step in their steps in case someone is wise enough to notice.

My one confidence is that unless Christian's health failed, he is still alive. Why guard a dead body? I push the tarp aside and step between the opening, letting it close behind me. Candles are burning on the altar. Feet stick out from behind the alter. A body.

The decaying body of a dead robed priest. I'm not super religious, but I'm pretty sure whoever did that is going straight to hell.   I hear voices.

They are speaking in Spanish. I understand them.   They are talking about going to get something to eat and sound frustrated at having to stay in here. They are walking toward the main doors.

I step behind the alter so burning candles will not cast my shadow. I bend down and my injured leg gives out and bumps the alter. The candles move and the flames flicker. They stop walking. They are coming toward the alter.

"Quien! Who's there!" a guard yells with a heavy accent.

Yeah, I will answer that. I stay as still as possible. No confrontation. Path of least resistance. I want an easy in and out. Then I hear it. The plastic is shoved aside and one man is approaching the left of the altar, the other approaches on the right. I lay flat on my back. The altar is on legs. I aim at the foot approaching on my left.

"Jose, Guillermo!" yells someone from the church doors.

They stop walking, and the feet turn, facing the main door.

"Yeah! Que? What do you want? You have food?" the man who almost lost a foot yells back.

"No, you Guapó. Fathead. Come-on, they need us up the street! Hurry!" he yells to them.

They shove the plastic tarp aside, and I hear the door close.

I stand, bracing myself on the altar. My leg is stiff. The door must be here. But where? I look down at the floor. The drag marks lead to the wall. Odd? There it is. A secret door.

Hidden by carvings and blended to look like part of the wall art. There is no handle, it must be a spring door. I push it and it pops open.

Now, I'm wondering about Christian's condition. There is no guard here. He must be very weak to be no threat or drugged. A sinking feeling drops to my stomach. He could be dead.

As long as Christian's clients think he's alive, that's all Gutierrez needs. To make it look as if Christian is alive. He could just stash the body.

I don't want to hear those words spinning in my head. The words I will have to say to Tempest. I have told no one that someone they love is dead. Never. I don't want to have to do it.

There is a short hall about four feet long and I see an opening to the right. I take a deep breath, gun drawn. There may be someone with him. I turn the corner and can barely see a thing. There is a slit of window running horizontally high above the table. The light coming in lands right on the face of whoever walks in the room.

I can make out a long table. Like a communion table. I blink quickly, forcing my eyes to adjust. There is something, no, someone on it. A body is laying on it. It is a large man and his right arm dangles lifelessly from the table.

No. I lower my gun. I don't even know him, but his rescue, entrusted to me. I saw this man alive. I can't save all the people that were captured, but this one is on me. I feel the weight of his death is resting on my shoulders.

Maybe if I didn't get Tempest first. Jason is waiting to hear from me, but I can't bring myself to make that call. Not yet. I walk to Christian and put my hand on his chest. Wait. He's warm.

I take a pulse. It's faint, but he has one. I put the gun down on the table, pull open his eyelids and quietly slap his face on both cheeks, trying to rouse him. I pull up his sleeve. I thought so. Needle marks. They gave him something. There is no way I can lift him. I need him to wake up. The adrenaline syringes. I unzip my leather jacket and pull it out of the inner pocket.

"Here we go, Christian. You'll never forget this trip." I pop the cap and pause.

Truly, I don't want to give him this. I don't know how it will react with his heart. But if we stay here any longer, they will come back, move him or torture him... or kill him.

I look closely at his face. His left eye is swollen, and fresh blood is on his temple. Still in his traveling clothes. His wrists bloody from the handcuffs. His leather sandals are new and match the belt on his linen pants with a matching top.

I stick the syringe into the vein on his left arm and suppress the plunger slightly. I don't want to give him much, just enough. Enough to get him to wake. Nothing.

I give him more. He's up. It took more than I thought. I feel myself smile, rub my hair back and put the syringe down.

He gasps for air and sits straight up as if he were underwater. I put my hand on his back and brace him, just in case he drops backward. He looks at me and lands a right hook on my left jaw.

Man, that hurt. What the h...? I will blow that off as a freak reflex.

"Christian, some right hook. I'm here to get you out." I say rubbing my jaw, feeling my stubble on my cheek and chin as I step away from the table.

Christian squints and tries to look around the darkroom. He's still unstable. Swaying slightly. His left eye is bloodshot.

"Who are you? Where am I?" his robust voice shocks me.

"Caleb and you're in a Church," I say. He focuses on dusty cleric's robes hanging on the wall with a rosary beside them. He has a personality, a presence that feels friendly. Kind. It's the same feeling I got when I met Tempest. Familiar. The type of people you want to have dinner with and send Christmas cards to. "Can you walk?"

"I don't think so. My head." Christian says laying back down on the table.

"No, we have to move. Now." I say.

Voices. They are getting louder and coming toward the door. It's the guards. Why are they back? I hear a paper bag rustling. Maybe his food?

I look around the room. I can't take the chance of a shoot-out in these close quarters. Not with Christian in here. Besides, I wanted an easy in and out. I run my hand over my hair and look around the room for another out.

Zip my leather jacket steady my leg. All is silent except for distant protests. A cloud moved over the moon, giving us the advantage of extra darkness in the room. Tempest must be praying.

I close my eyes and listen. In this pitch blackness, they won't help me, anyway. The creek of the door opening. Footsteps enter slowly. Two men.

One man is wearing way too much cologne. The other, a lag in his step. He approaches, groping for the table. His hands tap the stack of cleric robes piled on top of me. He pulls something out, and I hear liquid drip, like a syringe squirting. His stomach touches the table. Now.

I press nuzzle of my gun into his stomach and pull the trigger. He falls on top of me. The syringe drops to the floor. I'm lying on the table beneath the stack of cleric's robes to make myself the stature of Christian.

His body, now my bulletproof vest. The sound of the gunshot muffled but clear. Christian is standing in the dark corner across the room. The clouds move, revealing bright moonlight. It blinds his eyes.

He is heading straight for the table. The weight of the body on me prevents my aim. I can't pull the trigger unless I'm sure Christian is not within range. I cannot miss it. Then I hear it.

Gurgling. I shove the body off of me and see Christian with his arm around the guard's neck. His muscular arm clenches him tightly. A few futile tugs at Christian's arm and the guard's body is limp. Christian releases his arm but gently lowers the guard's body to the floor with care. As if he were an injured friend.

I shove the dead guard's body and robes off of me and

hop off the table and head toward the door. I feel him not behind me. I turn and watch him for a moment. He takes the guards' pulse with his two fingers on the man's neck. I'm surprised.

That man was his captor. That man probably tortured Christian. They left him in this dungeon room, closed in and drugged him. Hot, alone, and he takes time to check his pulse? Already, this man is teaching me a silent but valuable lesson.

"Alive?" I ask.

"Yes," Christian says with relief.

"You really are a Christian." I joke.

I've done much worst. Christian stand and staggers slightly. I reach forward and steady him.

"We need to move. I have a plane waiting." I say ushering him out the door.

Christian looks at me, and it is profound. He looked past my eyes and taps something deeper.

"I didn't trust you before enough to ask. But, I do now. My wife. She's here in Mexico. She's alone."

I walk him through the door, and the plastic hanging in front of the alter. We reach the back door.

"Tempest is safe." I look him in the eye purposely when I said it.

If he doesn't believe she's safe, I cannot get this man on the plane.

"All right."   He nods.

I used her first name purposely.   Knowing him, he didn't use it, purposely.   I look at my watch.   We're running out of time.   Moving steadily and silently, we reach the back door.   It is locked.

CAPTURED

CHAPTER FIFTEEN

If my calculations are right, Gutierrez is having his men breach the President of Mexico's private residence. The coup has begun.

The President's military will follow Gutierrez's orders, thinking the orders are coming from the President. Gutierrez's will order them to attack the loyal followers of Ruiz. At that point, the military will have to decide in whom their loyalties lay. Valkyrie. The tactic used by Hitler's high officials to seize control before they were attacked to show the world that not all of them stood with Hitler.

I put a failsafe in position. I don't have to wonder who he will be loyal to. He's loyal to the money. He and his men are to establish a perimeter around President Ruiz's residence and hold.

I can't shoot the lock and risk being heard. I kick the plywood door, and it splits in the center. Gun first, in steady military form stance, I step through the broken door and look both ways down the alley.

A guard on the left and one on the right aim and shoot at me. I pull the trigger. Click. I'm empty. I step back into the doorway and push Christian against the stone wall in the corner. The guard's gun comes through the doorway first.

I grab the muzzle, bend his elbow and turn the gun to his face.   His impulse, he pulls the trigger. One-shot to the head and his body drops. I pull the gun from his hand, two shots to the chest of the other guard coming in right behind him.

"Move!"   I yell to Christian.

We exit the building and head toward the street in the opposite direction of the chaos. The darkness is lifting. The sunrise is peaking out in the distance at the end of the street. I glance at my watch. If all goes as planned, the President of Mexico's private residence is surrounded. Surrounded by my men.

I need to call him once we get clear. We move swiftly. Christian is keeping up well, but I'm watching him. He's winded. I break the driver's side window on a vehicle. The tempered glass showers on the driver's seat. Christian is leaning on the passenger side door.

"You're stealing it?"   he says over the noise of the rioting up the block.

"Get in,"   I say.

"This isn't your car."   He says.

"Christian, we need to go. Get in the car."

"The owner will wake up tomorrow to go to work and not have their car."

I can't believe this. He's an imposing character. If this man doesn't want to budge, he won't. I admire his integrity, but if I thought I could, I'd drag him into this car right now. I hear boots coming.

"I'll send it back. All right. I'll bring it back. Get in the car, Christian."

He looks at me, checking for my honesty. He sees it. He gets into the car. A pair of baby shoes dangle from the rear-view mirror. I look at Christian staring at them then, at me. I snatch the shoes down.

"I'll bring it back." I start the car.

We need to get to the airstrip, fast.

Christian is silent. A few blocks later, I have to ask.

"Christian, you were kidnapped, beaten, and separated from your wife on your second honeymoon but you… you didn't want to kill them, you don't want to use a car that's not yours to escape. Did they give you… something?" I ask.

He looks straight ahead and smiles slightly. The corners of his eyes go up. He's the man you would gravitate to talk to even in a crowded room. The one you call to your side when your heartbroken or in need. There is a humble calm on him. I know very little about Christian, but one thing I am sure of, Wallie was right. This man is worth saving.

There is an unspoken presence with him I only caught a whiff of before. What is it? Who else gave me this... feeling? That's it. The Archbishop.

His chest is heaving. I don't like that. I glance at my cell phone. I'm expecting something from President Ruiz.

"Mexico did not do this to me. A few people don't represent the whole but if I do to them, what they did to me, how am I a Christian?"

"You hit me pretty decent... for a Christian." Humorously trying to poke a hole in his theory.

"That was the injection, not me." He laughs. "A man should live remembering he has to answer for his deeds one day. That's what I believe, anyway."

"You preaching to me, Christian?"

I say, glancing in the rear-view mirror as I drive.

"Just sharing what worked for me..." his head bobs slightly, "... Caleb, do you know the meaning of your name?" he asks.

His strong robust voice wavers slightly. I try to look at his face and keep my eyes on the road. He's purposely diverting his face from my view. Why? I want to keep him talking.

"No, I don't. What does it mean?" I ask him.

"Promise me you will look it up. All right, Caleb Promise? And promise me you will take me to my calm waters."

He's rambling now. What... calm waters? I press the gas. The car speeds up. I stamp on the accelerator. It hits the floor of the car and can't go any further. My heart is racing. My breath is short. I promised Tempest. He can't die. I call Jason and put the phone on speaker on the dashboard.

"Put the President on."

"He's not just going to come to the phone, Caleb! He doesn't even know about you." Jason asks eagerly.

"Tell the President, I have Christian Bleu and if he wants to know what else I know, he will take this call," I say.

It's amazing what fear can instigate.

Sirens sound. Crowds are seeping into the streets. "THE PRESIDENT IS DEAD. Long live President Gutierrez!" Someone yells.

I reach over and put my two fingers on Christian's left wrist. His arm is limp. I can't find it. Wait... is that a beat? Jerking the steering wheel left to right, avoiding groups of protesters dotting the street. Yes. It's there. Faint, but there.

"This is the President. Mr. Promise. I understand you have something to tell me."

"I do, Mr. President. First, may I ask you a question?"

"We are in the middle of a situation. We are about to extract the bodies of our embassy workers."

"You mean the eight bodies alive in the bunker in the basement that Christian Bleu designed? The eight instructed precisely when to go in there, just before our bomb exploded. The bomb planted by one of the United States embassy guards. An order you issued? Those bodies?"

He is silent. Importantly, there is no denial.

"What message do you have for me? Time is of the essence."

"I'm not rich, I don't have stuff I need to hide so well that I have to hire someone like Christian here, but what I have, is the knowledge that President Ruiz was not involved. Gutierrez took Christian. He hired gangs to abduct U. S. Citizens to incite an attack from us. Gutierrez incited a coup. He wants the Presidency.

He wants you to do exactly what you are doing. Engage. People will grab a leader, even a bad one, if they are afraid. He has made them afraid of war."

"Personal matters of another country are not our concern. Once those coffins rise from that burnt embassy in plain sight, this deal closes."

"And you go up in the poles, Sir."

I look in my rearview mirror. The Black hawk shines its spotlight into the gaping hole in the embassy roof and lowers a thick steel cable.

"This is not the course of action I want to take, Mr. Promise. American lives are at stake. We can make no other country presume abducting Americans will be tolerated."

"I get it. Look, make your point in your next term. Handle this right, you're guaranteed it. This was that of one man. Christian is safe. We may explain the explosion as an accident. Ruiz will bring Gutierrez to justice, and you, viewed as the peacemaker. You can walk softly and carry a big stick."

"I'm sorry, Mr. Promise. Your time is up." Says the President.

I don't know what Christian knows or has access to about him, but it is big. Big enough for him to bomb an embassy. Big enough for him to risk breaking policy to get him back.

I look in the rearview mirror. Two black vehicles are speeding up behind us. They are on our trail. Who are they?

"Give me the phone." Says Christian softly.

I didn't know he was conscious. I hand it to him and steady the car jolting from large pot-holes in the street.

"Mr. President..." he whispers.

I can't hear what he is saying. His voice is faint. Both hands on the wheel. I am driving as fast as this car will go on a straight road. People jump out in front of the car every few feet. A small thump.

The cell phone slipped from Christian's open hand, resting palm upon his thigh.

"No, no, no... come on!" I hit the car horn to clear the road.

Too far from the embassy site now. I can't see what is happening. If a body container raises on that line, it's done. A strike is imminent.

Shots. Someone is shooting at us. The bullets hit the trunk with a thud. I have to get Christian to the plane, but they need to be gone first.

Undeniably, the President's motivating factor to issue the order to have the eight embassy workers taken out in the body containers is far more purposeful than my suggestion.

But what exactly did Christian say to him? Did the President even hear it? I can't reach the phone and steer at the same time.

The car is trying to pull up beside us on Christian's side. I swerve right. He swings around to the rear and comes up on my right. I drop back, slowing down slightly, keeping his site line staggered.

The driver looks at me and slows too. The armed passenger aims into the car and shoots. The bullet lodged in my headrest. He is where I want him. I speed up. The driver hits the gas, locking his eyes on me, oblivious to the forklift parked in front of him.

The one forklift arm bursts through the windshield,

piercing the chest of the driver. The other pins the passenger to his seat. One down, one more to go.

Christian slumps in his seat. Reach over him and pull his seatbelt, securing him in his seat. In the side-view mirror, the passenger stands in the sunroof and is lifting something out. What is that? A rocket launcher!

This is not Gutierrez's men. They would try to get Christian back alive. Are they a gift from the U.S.? A cleanup team? Jason wouldn't do that, or would he? Me not knowing for certain solidifies my new decision.

Finally, I can see the airstrip. Serpentine. I drive swerving left to right not giving him a clear shot. He sways in the sunroof like a ping-pong ball. I pull open the glove compartment. A gun. Only two bullets.

An abandoned airplane hanger is open. It's an unfinished construction project. Zig-zag driving is tossing Christian side to side. Can't do this much longer. A pop and white smoke streams from my hood.

"COME-ON!"

I rock forward on the steering wheel. If I can get him on the plane just up the tarmac, he's got a chance. There is a medic aboard.

The man with the rocket launcher is swaying. I'm heading into the hanger. He has us locked in his sites. I drive straight through the hanger. I can't zig-zag.

Almost out of the hanger. A crane suspends four rusted beams is in front of us. I lift my foot off of the accelerator. Aim. Fire once. The bullet breaks one cable. The beams sway and drop slightly. Last one. I fire the second bullet. The last cable breaks.

The rusty beams release. I hit the gas. The beams pierce their roof, go through the driver's lap and lodge the car to the ground. Splints of rust shower on the car. Final two beams strike. One through the gas tank.

I pull the wheel. Hard left, putting us back on the tarmac. The gas tank explodes. A plume of fire. Then the rocket in the launcher blows. The force shoves our car forward. I put my arm across Caleb's chest, pressing him to the seat. In the rearview mirror, I see the doors of their vehicle car spinning mid-air and fall to the ground.

We head toward the plane. The door is open. The car Tempest and Jeff rode in is there.

"Talk to me, Christian! Come-on!"

The medic runs down the airplane steps. I swing the car right, putting Christian's door at the foot of the plane steps. He's the best medic I could get. Wartime experience.

If we get him to a hospital in time, he will have a better chance of living. My mind is reeling with what I could have done differently. What I should have done differently.

When a man stops questioning his actions, he has reached pride. And pride always comes before a fall. I don't want fall. He's unconscious. His chin has dropped, eyes still shut.

CHAPTER SIXTEEN

The medic leans over Christian with his stethoscope and puts his medical bag down on the ground, feeling for a pulse.

"Give me some room here."   He says to me.

I think he just doesn't want me here if Christian dies. The medics creased eyes concerned. Catching his hint, I pick the phone up off of the car floor and step out of the vehicle.

I back away from the car whose engine is smoking. My leg is stiff. Just as I catch my breath, Tempest steps into the plane's doorway.

She sees Christian, her knees wobble. She braces herself in the plane's doorway and her hand drifts to her mouth. The medic is actively attending to him.

She walks down the steps slowly and her face draws pale. She glances at me leaning on the car just for a moment. Yet, her expression will stay with me for the rest of my life. I know that look. Something broke in her.

Another medic comes out of the plane. After a few

moments, Christian is conscious. They assist him onto the plane. I watch the door close and it taxi's down the runway and takes off safely. I exhale. I'm not very religious, but today I will pray. I'll pray for that man. I get it. I see why they trust him. I trust him too.

I get into the overheated car and flip to the news on my phone, showing a helicopter raising a coffin-sized container through the open embassy roof. Tightly squeezing the steering wheel, I feel my jaw tighten. In the distant trees, a flicker of light. Binoculars? Gun?

I need to leave before my hidden visitor takes a shot at me. I have a feeling he wanted Christian dead. Me, he could have already killed.

Driving for the main road, I call Jason.

"Is he secured?" he asks.

Perhaps those weren't his men. He's not surprised to hear from me.

"I see the President did it, anyway. Can't say I'm surprised." I say.

I turn my face toward the rising Mexican sun on my left. It was a long night.

"Yeah, Jason. The package is secure. So that wasn't you trying to clean house?"

"Clean house? No. What do you take me for, Caleb? Was it Mexico?"

"Not likely. Why didn't you tell me the explosion was us?"

"You think they tell me everything?" I hear him chewing a pill. "Things around here are on a need-to-know basis. I didn't need to know, and neither did you. What were you doing poking around in the embassy, anyway? You had a job. I have a job. Do that. Nothing more, nothing less. Trust me, it saves you a headache in the long run."

"I was trying to save lives! Not just one life." He's walking as he speaks. The phone jostling slightly and he sounds breathless. He whispers. "for the record, what you did was the 'right' thing to do but you and I don't get to decide what's right. I follow orders because I'm a part of an entity bigger than myself." Says Jason.

"I don't belong to you!" Saying that aloud was freeing. I didn't realize I felt indebted to him.

"You are on the payroll, I'm not. I took this mission to save lives. My motives crystal clear. If you call me, know that I will exercise my freedom to decide what's right or wrong. The day I give that up, I'm not Caleb Promise."

"There is something bigger brewing, Caleb. Even bigger than your freedom. Gretchen didn't give him up. We found proof. Whoever was behind the Beaston is all over this case too. This guy doesn't play by anyone's rules. He's going after nations by pressing tempting those closest to the ones with power. We are close. We just-"

"-Stop! Jason, you're addicted."

Someone in the background calls Jason.

"Mr. Jones, the President will see you now." She says.

"We will talk about this later, Caleb, all right?" he pleads.

In my gut, I should say no. But one thing I know about Jason, he has an instinct and mostly, his intentions are good. I feel he is about to walk into a Presidential grilling.

"Caleb, all right? For me."

"All right. We'll talk later." I say.

He exhales.

"Thank you."

"Jason."

"Yes?"

"The President will ask you if I'm trustworthy. He's wondering if his secrets are safe. Say what you truly think. And stop eating those pills." I hang up the phone.

My work here is almost complete. I have to find Jeff's wife's body and return the car, as promised. I always keep a promise.

Driving back to where I got the car, my phone rings. It's President Ruiz of Mexico.

"Hello, Mr. President... still," I say jokingly.

"Yes still my friend, still." He chuckles. "I never imagined Gutierrez would have been the one. I want you to know that while in custody, he divulged the locations of the missing U. S. Citizens. Gutierrez offered their location, hoping for a leniency. He promised to pay the captors with hostage ransom. There will be no leniency for his crimes."

"The United States President will be glad to hear that," I say.

"How did you know he would reveal his position in front of the cameras at the embassy?"

"It was the one thing he truly wanted. The one thing that tempted him, was the chance to shine while the world watched. I did it so you would have no doubts. Eventually, it would have happened. I just sped up the process by releasing him in the right circumstances."

"Have you found what you came for?" he asks.

A double-edged question. I came here for Christian and I got much more. A greater understanding of my purpose and my convictions. An admiration for a man and his wife.

"I did. All the best to you, Sir."

"And to you, Mr. Caleb Promise." He hangs up

the phone.

"Just, Caleb," I say aloud to myself.

Is the person sitting in the wings sent by the mystery mastermind? The one Gretchen, from my first mission, refused to divulge. Could one person have had his or her hand in that mission and this one? War between countries was Gretchen's directive. A war between Mexico and the United States would have been imminent. The similarities are uncanny.

I reach for the car door handle and the phone Jason gave me slips from my hand hitting the concrete. The back pops off. I pick it up to put it back on and my thumb runs over a scrawled engraving. "MI-6". What is Jason up to? He wanted me to find this.

I stick a stack of cash under the driver's seat cover. More than enough to buy another car. I park it in its spot, get out and shut the door walking away. The streets filled with Ruiz's supporters celebrating. I get a feeling I haven't felt in years. A desire to go home. To climb onto the sofa in the tank and watch the fireplace. Perhaps because until now, nowhere felt like home. Hot shower, a cold swim and just sit down there in this space made for me, away from everything else and sleep.

There is a lot to sort out. I don't know if Christian will survive, and the murder of Jeff's wife doesn't sit well with me at all.

Right now, Jason is assuring the President that I'm no snitch. It's for his gain. He'll preserve his reputation and judgement of character. To stain me would stain himself.

One Week Later

United States

The President of the United States waited until all the missing citizens returned to the United States then, he issued a statement that it was sensitive documents that survived the explosion lifted in those caskets sized containers retrieved from the embassy. He was certain to play that alongside footage of the hostages tearfully greeting their families. His ratings shot through the roof. The tail end of his speech. was textbook worthy.

"It is vital that going forward, all citizens of the United States know that I will do everything possible to ensure their safety as they travel around this world and to maintain the stable and sure-footed actions we as a nation are known for. Thank you and God bless the United States of America."

I find nothing comforting about a cemetery. Standing beneath this perfectly trimmed tree, rain sliding down my leather jacket, she saw me. This is as close as I will come. Returning Nancy's body to the states for burial for Jeff made me think about tipping points. Things like this take people to their tipping point. Yet, he stands there. Collected. Calm. Holding Tempest's hand as they lower Christian's casket into the ground.

I didn't really break the vow Wallie, and I made years ago after my parent's funeral. We vowed that would be the last funeral we ever attended. I'm here, but not here. I needed Tempest to see me, but what I see troubles my waters. She steps out from beneath the covering of the oversized umbrella into the rain, takes off her hat and turns her face up, letting the rain drench her face and hair. Odd? Perhaps it's shock. My gut tells me that Tempest Bleu has reached her tipping point.

CHAPTER SEVENTEEN
BEYOND THE BOOK

Get new release deals, free books and any promotional give-aways coming up. I respect your email box and only send things I feel you want to know about.

What you'll get...

Monthly Newsletter
Book Promotions
Pre-Release Offers
New Book Release Deals & Give-aways.
Type the link below into your browser:

https://www.kabryant.com/join-mailer

Join free with one click.

Jumping into that other world priceless. Hot cup in hand, I started writing for the love of writing and can't think of anything I would rather do for the rest of my life. Once a writer, always a writer. A vision grew to draw a leisure reader, confined patient, or a child on summer vacation with their feet twirling in the grass, into a new world between two covers. I want to invite you to join the mailing list to stay informed of all the new upcoming promotions and book give-away.

Type the link in your browser:
https://www.kabryant.com/copy-of-books

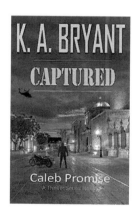

FOR READERS, BLOGGERS, POD-CASTERS, YOU-TUBERS AND BOOK REVIEWERS

SPECIAL OFFER:

Reviews are a tremendous influence on-line, and it would really help me reach my writing goal if you would write a quick review.   Your feedback tells me what you want to see more or less of.

I can write it, but I need you to push it.   If you are a Blogger, Pod-Castor, You-Tuber or Book Reviewer, I invite you to join the street team.   A vetted influencer can get pre-launch peeks at books.

I believe we never stop learning.   It's a lifelong gift to grow and change.

Type the link in your bowser:

https://www.kabryant.com/street-team-sign-up

K.A. BRYANT, Author

I still remember how warm it was in Mrs. Harris's English class. She liked it that way although she wore a sweater. I don't know why I was always distracted by her long beaded necklaces she pulled on habitually. That was when teachers wore silk blouses, long skirts down to their mid calf with stockings and shoes that clicked when they walked.

She was a retired play-write with her passion for the written word evident in her detailed critique of every short story scrawled by the twenty children in the class. She was the catalyst. The pointed finger saying 'go that way'. All I knew was it was fun. Oh, the simple thinking era.

Life, time and the Internet soon showed me that there was so much more to writing. The wonderful thing was discovering a world of wonderful people with either a love of reading, writing, or both so willing to share their opinions and be a pointed finger.

Much time has passed since Mrs. Harris's class, but I'm still going in the direction of that pointed finger.

My hope... is that my journey in writing will find my books in the hands of readers all over the world and inspire someone to reach further, write more, or just explore their dream. Hope can be lost when you are going through a long, seemingly endless difficult time, just as the main character Caleb Promise experienced. In the book, keeping focused on his mission pulled him out of the pit-experience he was in. An experience that was draining him of his strength and willingness to live.

You and I... can propel a vision past expectations. I can write it, but I need you to read it, write a review and if you liked it, recommend it to a friend. You can stay in touch with me by Twitter @kabryantauthor, Facebook @kabryantbooks. I am also on Instagram, GoodReads, and WordPress. If you enjoy the books and blogs, you can show your support on Patreon.com.

Thank you for reading the book!

CHAPTER EIGHTEEN
Sneak Peak of a Book

MARK OF THE TWO-EDGED SWORD

Description

At fifteen, a car accident killed Caleb Promise's parents. Mysterious? Normally not, but when your father was the master strategist for an under-cover military strike team and the sole survivor of a mission-gone-bad, his death is definitely mysterious. The old stone monastery orphanage behind him, Caleb is wrapped in bitterness and entangled in trying to finish his father's final mission. The promise for embarking on this treacherous mission? Finding his parents murderer and destroying a mysterious living weapon of mass destruction called the Beaston.

Assassins on his heels, time is running out. Can he overcome his personal issues to figure out the clues his father left him. Clues encrypted in their relationship. His father's clues, along with his drive can cut through layers of deception to the core... like a two-edged sword. If he succeeds, they will leave their mark, the Mark of the Two-Edged Sword.

CHAPTER ONE

CALEB PROMISE
New York

The tree isn't wide enough, not nearly wide enough. It never is. Right now, being a man that is six foot two inches, isn't helping. My broad shoulders are sticking out. I can feel it. It's going to see me. Maybe if I crouch. It isn't finished yet. Not even close. The sound of my heart pounding seems louder than their screams, and it hears everything. That's how it found them underground in that muddy tunnel covered by the fall leaves.

They hid for weeks. A group here, a group there. Don't ask me how I know, I just do. Thin, rationing food for months. I can hear them praying as it holds them up like trophies in front of the government vehicle's lights. The agents, bored now, slump in their seats. The cold frost of their breath glows in the headlights.

Taller than any human, the face of a lioness and arms of a gorilla. That's all I ever see. It fades into shadows. No matter how hard I try, I never see all of it. Why am I always barefoot?

People who don't have this think it's cool, but it's not. Consciousness in a dream used to be fun. The ability to choose which way to go, whether to fly or walk and even to wake up or not. It's not fun. I don't truly rest. Ever. Especially in this dream. It has returned every night for weeks.

I've got to try to make it to that rock without it hearing me. From there, I may be able to see it. All of it. There she is, the lady with the red hair. The creature turns around right after pulling her out. This is my chance.

I take one step. It's over. I felt it crack beneath my foot. My eyes close, praying it didn't hear me. But I know it did. I open my eyes, it's staring right at me.

It opens its claw, releasing her. It's coming. The ground vibrates with each step. I can't hear anything except my heart pounding. She's falling to the ground, but the drop encompasses me.

I jolt awake. Sitting straight up. My room is as cold and clammy as the dream. It's over, but the eeriness of the dream hangs in the air with the feeling that someone else was in that forest. Someone watches with a disconnected heart. Alive enough, but uncaring. Unaffected by what they saw.

A shiver runs up my back. The cheap flat coverlet in my grip lost its usefulness months ago. Now it only keeps the roaches from falling on my sheets.

I had no choice. This is where the orphanage arranged for me to live after I turned eighteen. It has been three years now living in this hotel-style living quarter. Wow, it seems as if I've been here much longer than that. I feel older than that. I don't want to get up yet.

I give in, flop back onto the flat dingy pillow and draw the cover up to my chin. My full beard and hair soaked from perspiration. The rubber band I used to tie my hair back for work last night is now poking me in the ear.

It won't be long now. The shivering has begun and even with my eyes closed, the room spins violently and my head is pulsing.

CAPTURED

"Shut up!" I yell.

The neighbors on the other side of the thin wall are always fighting. Every morning a blaring argument with their morning coffee about why he came home so late.

"You shut up!" She yells back with two bangs on the wall, making the cheap framed photo above my head jump.

The pulsing turns into a full-blown blinding headache. I have to get up. I don't want to, but I have no choice. There it is, the chalky aspirin in the back of the night table drawer, right beside my keys and an unopened Gideon Bible. Flat soda works just at well, washing it down as a glass of cold water. I stagger into the bathroom. Funny, there's no heat, but the hot water in the shower works perfectly.

One advantage to being taller than average, I can reach the loose screws to the rusted vent in the wall easily. My hiding place. My fingers fumble around in the vent, searching for it. There it is. The dusty black sock guarding my life savings. The knot is smaller than last month. It started shrinking when my dream started shrinking.

I can't help but give it a squeeze right before I put it away, sort of mental measurement of how much I have to put back if I ever regain hope of getting out of here. Where is the key? There, inside a fold in the sock, I feel it. A small gold-tone key. I rub its outline between my fingers. It is a lifeline to reality. I have a feeling I'll be needing it soon.

I started saving money the week I began work. I started work the day after the orphanage driver dropped me at the front door, a wide-eyed country boy gazing at sky scrapers.

Manhattan is full of lavish apartments with doormen tipping their hats as residents walk in swinging shiny shopping bags. Fresh out of the orphanage, I honestly believed that could be me one day swinging those bags.

Hope. A gift from my parents. They always told me I could do and be anything. They told me I was smart and like any kid; I believed what my parents said. I never imagined the best I could be was the one holding the door. They never got to finish me. It's not their fault.

I can still remember the dress my mother wore to my fifteenth birthday party just three days before she and my father were killed in the accident. At least then, I thought it was an accident. I can't think about that right now.

Housekeeping is coming today. Nothing spurs change like three police raids and a threat to be shut down. They knock on the door like the police. Hard and loud. When I open the door, if she doesn't suspect anything, she hands me clean sheets and towels. If it's tied, she'll take the trash.

However, if she has suspicions, she does a thorough 'cleaning' of the room. I noticed a pattern. These were no petite housekeepers wearing uniform dresses and nursing shoes. They always wore jeans and were more muscular than most men, with a pistol bulging in the small of their back.

The press-board dresser with sharp corners holds the residue of every meal I ate for the week. I can hear the three knocks of the housekeeper getting louder as she comes up the hall. I fold the pizza boxes and deli bags into the garbage can.

In the bottom of the can, my empty bottles. They clank in the can, telling my life's story. The faster I move, the more the torn linoleum snags the bottom of my socks. I can't help but look at the crack in the corner of the large rectangular dresser mirror. It's not supposed to be there, maybe that's why it keeps catching my eye. It's the flaw in perfection. I thought of covering it, but it's got a right to be there, just like the rest of the mirror.

I'm tired. At twenty-one, I'm tired. Tired of being the crack in the mirror. I've been mistaken for being in my forties. Tiredness makes you look old and feel old.

A flash of light outside of my window draws my attention. The 'C' outside of my window was the first one in neon 'Vacancy' sign running vertically down the building and it is lit. It wasn't lit yesterday. She's here. Three loud bangs.

"Housekeeping."

I knot the top of the full garbage bag, drop it on the floor beside the door, and open the door. Bare-face, she looks at me emotionless. I snatch the sheets off of the bed into a ball and hold them out to her. She looks past me into the room. She isn't taken aback by my lean undershirt-clad physique.

She pushes past me, glances into the bathroom then drops the stack of clean sheets with towels on the bed. With gloved hands, she grabs the sheets from my hands and her cold stare reflects just how much she loves her job. One foot in the hall, she drops the sheets into the cart and grabs the garbage bag and walks out, leaving the door open behind her. A real ray of sunshine.

I look down at myself, sort of wondering why she wasn't in awe. I have a crease in my pants and everything. The cleaner's crease is always stiff and the pant bottoms are wide enough to go over my black boots. I walk to the door to close it.

Out of habit, I look left and right down the hall before closing the door. She starts pushing the over-sized cart to the next room. My sarcasm gets the best of me. After all, it's almost been a full five hours.

"And a Merry Christmas to you." I say.

As expected, she ignores me, rolling to the next room, but she pauses, she looks toward the floor to her left. What's over there? The cart passes revealing the hall prostitute with eyes dripping in makeup, knees drawn into her chest and back pressed to the wall of her pimp's apartment. A labored exhale.

I fell prey to her once. Not the way most would. One glance at those glazed eyes, bleach blond hair and it all came back. My ignorance. She's about my age. I felt bad for her. That night, the hall was dark, hot and smelly and I still had my streak of naivete fresh off the farm. I invited her in, offered her hot pizza and a cool breeze under my oscillating fan for the night. I gave her the bed and slept on the floor.

I woke to a boot in my gut and watched her willingly obey her large under dressed pimp to rob me of my last forty-five dollars. I know why she did it. It wasn't for the obvious reason. I look at it as payment for what she brought with her.

Keep reading… Get:

MARK OF THE TWO-EDGED SWORD

Available where books are sold.
Type into your browser:
https://www.kabryant.com

Printed in Great Britain
by Amazon

86450688R00166